Charles Dickens

A Message from the Sea

Charles Dickens

A Message from the Sea

ISBN/EAN: 9783743435605

Printed in Europe, USA, Canada, Australia, Japan

Cover: Foto ©Andreas Hilbeck / pixelio.de

More available books at **www.hansebooks.com**

A
MESSAGE FROM THE SEA.

THE EXTRA CHRISTMAS NUMBER OF **ALL THE YEAR ROUND.**

CONDUCTED BY CHARLES DICKENS.

CONTAINING THE AMOUNT OF TWO ORDINARY NUMBERS.

CHRISTMAS, 1860.

Price
4d.

CHAPTER I. THE VILLAGE.

"AND a mighty sing'lar and pretty place it is, as ever I saw in all the days of my life!" said Captain Jorgan, looking up at it.

Captain Jorgan had to look high to look at it, for the village was built sheer up the face of a steep and lofty cliff. There was no road in it, there was no wheeled vehicle in it, there was not a level yard in it. From the sea-beach to the cliff-top, two irregular rows of white houses, placed opposite to one another, and twisting here and there and there and here, rose, like the sides of a long succession of stages of crooked ladders, and you climbed up the village or climbed down the village by the staves between: some six feet wide or so, and made of sharp irregular stones. The old pack-saddle, long laid aside in most parts of England as one of the appendages of its infancy, flourished here intact. Strings of pack-horses and pack-donkeys toiled slowly up the staves of the ladders, bearing fish, and coal, and such other cargo as was unshipping at the pier from the dancing fleet of village boats, and from two or three little coasting traders. As the beasts of burden ascended laden, or descended light, they got so lost at intervals in the floating clouds of village smoke, that they seemed to dive down some of the village chimneys and come to the surface again far off, high above others. No two houses in the village were alike, in chimney, size, shape, door, window, gable, roof-tree, anything. The sides of the ladders were musical with water, running clear and bright. The staves were musical with the clattering feet of the pack-horses and pack-donkeys, and the voices of the fishermen urging them up, mingled with the voices of the fishermen's wives and their many children. The pier was musical with the wash of the sea, the creaking of capstans and windlasses, and the airy fluttering of little vanes and sails. The rough sea-bleached boulders of which the pier was made, and the whiter boulders of the shore, were brown with drying nets. The red-brown cliffs, richly wooded to their extremest verge, had their softened and beautiful forms reflected in the bluest water, under the

clear North Devonshire sky of a November day without a cloud. The village itself was so steeped in autumnal foliage, from the houses giving on the pier, to the topmost round of the topmost ladder, that one might have fancied it was out a birds'-nesting, and was (as indeed it was) a wonderful climber. And mentioning birds, the place was not without some music from them too; for, the rook was very busy on the higher levels, and the gull with his flapping wings was fishing in the bay, and the lusty little robin was hopping among the great stone blocks and iron rings of the breakwater, fearless in the faith of his ancestors and the Children in the Wood.

Thus it came to pass that Captain Jorgan, sitting balancing himself on the pier-wall, struck his legs with his open hand, as some men do when they are pleased—and as he always did when he was pleased—and said:

"A mighty sing'lar and pretty place it is, as ever I saw in all the days of my life!"

Captain Jorgan had not been through the village, but had come down to the pier by a winding side-road, to have a preliminary look at it from the level of his own natural element. He had seen many things and places, and had stowed them all away in a shrewd intellect and a vigorous memory. He was an American born, was Captain Jorgan—a New Englander—but he was a citizen of the world, and a combination of most of the best qualities of most of its best countries.

For Captain Jorgan to sit anywhere in his long-skirted blue coat and blue trousers, without holding converse with everybody within speaking distance, was a sheer impossibility. So, the captain fell to talking with the fishermen, and to asking them knowing questions about the fishery, and the tides, and the currents, and the race of water off that point yonder, and what you kept in your eye, and got into a line with what else when you ran into the little harbour; and other nautical profundities. Among the men who exchanged ideas with the captain, was a young fellow, who exactly hit his fancy—a young fisherman of two or three-and-twenty, in the rough sea-dress of his craft, with a brown face, dark curling hair, and bright modest eyes under his Sou'-Wester hat, and with a frank but simple and retiring manner which the captain found uncommonly taking. "I'd bet a thousand dollars," said the captain to himself, "that your father was an honest man!"

"Might you be married now?" asked the captain when he had had some talk with this new acquaintance.

"Not yet."

"Going to be?" said the captain.

"I hope so."

The captain's keen glance followed the slightest possible turn of the dark eye, and the slightest possible tilt of the Sou'-Wester hat. The captain then slapped both his legs, and said to himself:

"Never knew such a good thing in all my life! There's his sweetheart looking over the wall!"

There was a very pretty girl looking over the wall, from a little platform of cottage, vine, and fuchsia; and she certainly did not look as if the presence of this young fisherman in the landscape, made it any the less sunny and hopeful for her.

Captain Jorgan, having doubled himself up to laugh with that hearty good nature which is quite exultant in the innocent happiness of other people, had undoubled himself and was going to start a new subject, when there appeared coming down the lower ladders of stones a man whom he hailed as "Tom Pettifer Ho!" Tom Pettifer Ho responded with alacrity, and in speedy course descended on the pier.

"Afraid of a sunstroke in England in November, Tom, that you wear your tropical hat, strongly paid outside and paper-lined inside, here?" said the captain, eyeing it.

"It's as well to be on the safe side, sir," replied Tom.

"Safe side!" repeated the captain, laughing. "You'd guard against a sunstroke with that old hat, in an Ice Pack. Wa'al! What have you made out at the Post-office?"

"It *is* the Post-office, sir."

"What's the Post-office?" said the captain.

"The name, sir. The name keeps the Post-office."

"A coincidence!" said the captain. "A lucky hit! Show me where it is. Good-by, shipmates, for the present! I shall come and have another look at you, afore I leave, this afternoon."

This was addressed to all there, but especially the young fisherman; so, all there acknowledged it, but especially the young fisherman. "*He's* a sailor!" said one to another, as they looked after the captain moving away. That he was; and so outspeaking was the sailor in him, that although his dress had nothing nautical about it with the single exception of its colour, but was a suit of a shore-going shape and form, too long in the sleeves, and too short in the legs, and too unaccommodating everywhere, terminating earthward in a pair of Wellington boots, and surmounted by a tall stiff hat which no

mortal could have worn at sea in any wind under Heaven; nevertheless, a glimpse of his sagacious weather-beaten face or his strong brown hand would have established the captain's calling. Whereas, Mr. Pettifer—a man of a certain plump neatness with a curly whisker, and elaborately nautical in a jacket and shoes and all things correspondent—looked no more like a seaman, beside Captain Jorgan, than he looked like a sea-serpent.

The two climbed high up the village—which had the most arbitrary turns and twists in it, so that the cobbler's house came dead across the ladder, and to have held a reasonable course you must have gone through his house, and through him too, as he sat at his work between two little windows, with one eye microscopically on the geological formation of that part of Devonshire, and the other telescopically on the open sea—the two climbed high up the village, and stopped before a quaint little house, on which was painted "MRS. RAYBROCK, DRAPER;" and also, "POST-OFFICE." Before it, ran a rill of murmuring water, and access to it was gained by a little plank-bridge.

"Here's the name," said Captain Jorgan, "sure enough. You can come in if you like, Tom."

The captain opened the door, and passed into an odd little shop about six feet high, with a great variety of beams and bumps in the ceiling, and, besides the principal window giving on the ladder of stones, a purblind little window of a single pane of glass: peeping out of an abutting corner at the sun-lighted ocean, and winking at its brightness.

"How do you do, ma'am?" said the captain. "I am very glad to see you. I have come a long way to see you."

"*Have* you, sir? Then I am sure I am very glad to see *you*, though I don't know you from Adam."

Thus, a comely elderly woman, short of stature, plump of form, sparkling and dark of eye, who, perfectly clean and neat herself, stood in the midst of her perfectly clean and neat arrangements, and surveyed Captain Jorgan with smiling curiosity. "Ah! but you are a sailor, sir," she added, almost immediately, and with a slight movement of her hands, that was not very unlike wringing them; "then you are heartily welcome."

"Thankee, ma'am," said the captain. "I don't know what it is, I am sure, that brings out the salt in me, but everybody seems to see it on the crown of my hat and the collar of my coat. Yes, ma'am, I am in that way of life."

"And the other gentleman, too," said Mrs. Raybrock.

"Well now, ma'am," said the captain, glancing shrewdly at the other gentleman, "you are that nigh right, that he goes to sea—if that makes him a sailor. This is my steward, ma'am, Tom Pettifer; he's been a'most all trades you could name, in the course of his life—would have bought all your chairs and tables once, if you had wished to sell 'em—but now he's

A MESSAGE FROM THE SEA.

my steward. My name's Jorgan, and I'm a shipowner, and I sail my own and my partners' ships, and have done so this five-and-twenty year. According to custom I am called Captain Jorgan, but I am no more a captain, bless your heart! than you are."

"Perhaps you'll come into my parlour, sir, and take a chair?" said Mrs. Raybrock.

"Ex-actly what I was going to propose myself, ma'am. After you."

Thus replying, and enjoining Tom to give an eye to the shop, Captain Jorgan followed Mrs. Raybrock into the little low back-room—decorated with divers plants in pots, tea-trays, old china teapots, and punch-bowls—which was at once the private sitting-room of the Raybrock family, and the inner cabinet of the post-office of the village of Steepways.

"Now, ma'am," said the captain, "it don't signify a cent to you where I was born, except——" But, here the shadow of some one entering, fell upon the captain's figure, and he broke off to double himself up, slap both his legs, and ejaculate, "Never knew such a thing in all my life! Here he is again! How are you?"

These words referred to the young fellow who had so taken Captain Jorgan's fancy down at the pier. To make it all quite complete he came in accompanied by the sweetheart whom the captain had detected looking over the wall. A prettier sweetheart the sun could not have shone upon, that shining day. As she stood before the captain, with her rosy lips just parted in surprise, her brown eyes a little wider open than was usual from the same cause, and her breathing a little quickened by the ascent (and possibly by some mysterious hurry and flurry at the parlour door, in which the captain had observed her face to be for a moment totally eclipsed by the Sou'-Wester hat), she looked so charming, that the captain felt himself under a moral obligation to slap both his legs again. She was very simply dressed, with no other ornament than an autumnal flower in her bosom. She wore neither hat nor bonnet, but merely a scarf or kerchief, folded squarely back over the head, to keep the sun off—according to a fashion that may be sometimes seen in the more genial parts of England as well as of Italy, and which is probably the first fashion of head-dress that came into the world when grasses and leaves went out.

"In my country," said the captain, rising to give her his chair, and dexterously sliding it close to another chair on which the young fisherman must necessarily establish himself—"in my country we should call Devonshire beauty, first-rate!"

Whenever a frank manner is offensive, it is because it is strained or feigned; for, there may be quite as much intolerable affectation in plainness, as in mincing nicety. All that the captain said and did, was honestly according to his nature; and his nature was open nature and good nature; therefore, when he paid this little compliment, and expressed with a sparkle or two of his knowing eye, "I see how it is, and nothing could be better," he had established a delicate confidence on that subject with the family.

"I was saying to your worthy mother," said the captain to the young man, after again introducing himself by name and occupation: "I was saying to your mother (and you're very like her) that it didn't signify where I was born, except that I was raised on question-asking ground, where the babies as soon as ever they come into the world, inquire of their mothers 'Neow, how old may you be, and wa'at air you a goin' to name me?'—which is a fact." Here he slapped his leg. "Such being the case, I may be excused for asking you if your name's Alfred?"

"Yes, sir, my name is Alfred," returned the young man.

"I am not a conjuror," pursued the captain, "and don't think me so, or I shall right soon undeceive you. Likewise don't think, if you please, though I do come from that country of the babies, that I am asking questions for question-asking's sake, for I am not. Somebody belonging to you, went to sea?"

"My elder brother Hugh," returned the young man. He said it in an altered and lower voice, and glanced at his mother: who raised her hands hurriedly, and put them together across her black gown, and looked eagerly at the visitor.

"No! For God's sake, don't think that!" said the captain, in a solemn way; "I bring no good tidings of him."

There was a silence, and the mother turned her face to the fire and put her hand between it and her eyes. The young fisherman slightly motioned towards the window, and the captain, looking in that direction, saw a young widow sitting at a neighbouring window across a little garden, engaged in needlework, with a young child sleeping on her bosom. The silence continued until the captain asked of Alfred:

"How long is it since it happened?"

"He shipped for his last voyage, better than three years ago."

"Ship struck upon some reef or rock, as I take it," said the captain, "and all hands lost?"

"Yes."

"Wa'al!" said the captain, after a shorter silence. "Here I sit who may come to the same end, like enough. He holds the seas in the hollow of His hand. We must all strike somewhere and go down. Our comfort, then, for ourselves and one another, is, to have done our duty. I'll wager your brother did his!"

"He did!" answered the young fisherman. "If ever man strove faithfully on all occasions to do his duty, my brother did. My brother was not a quick man (anything but that), but he was a faithful, true, and just man. We were the sons of only a small tradesman in this county, sir; yet our father was as watchful of his good name as if he had been a king."

"A precious sight more so, I hope—bearing in mind the general run of that class of crittur," said the captain. "But I interrupt."

"My brother considered that our father left the good name to us, to keep clear and true."

"Your brother considered right," said the captain; "and you couldn't take care of a better legacy. But again I interrupt."

"No; for I have nothing more to say. We know that Hugh lived well for the good name, and we feel certain that he died well for the good name. And now it has come into my keeping. And that's all."

"Well spoken!" cried the captain. "Well spoken, young man! Concerning the manner of your brother's death;" by this time, the captain had released the hand he had shaken, and sat with his own broad brown hands spread out on his knees, and spoke aside; "concerning the manner of your brother's death, it may be that I have some information to give you; though it may not be, for I am far from sure. Can we have a little talk alone?"

The young man rose; but, not before the captain's quick eye had noticed that, on the pretty sweetheart's turning to the window to greet the young widow with a nod and a wave of the hand, the young widow had held up to her the needle-work on which she was engaged, with a patient and pleasant smile. So the captain said, being on his legs:

"What might she be making now?"

"What is Margaret making, Kitty?" asked the young fisherman—with one of his arms apparently mislaid somewhere.

As Kitty only blushed in reply, the captain doubled himself up, as far as he could, standing, and said, with a slap of his leg:

"In my country we should call it wedding-clothes. Fact! We should, I do assure you."

But, it seemed to strike the captain in another light too; for, his laugh was not a long one, and he added in quite a gentle tone:

"And it's very pretty, my dear, to see her—poor young thing, with her fatherless child upon her bosom—giving up her thoughts to your home and your happiness. It's very pretty, my dear, and it's very good. May your marriage be more prosperous than hers, and be a comfort to her, too. May the blessed sun see you all happy together, in possession of the good name, long after I have done ploughing the great salt field that is never sown!"

Kitty answered very earnestly. "O! Thank you, sir, with all my heart!" And, in her loving little way, kissed her hand to him, and possibly by implication to the young fisherman too, as the latter held the parlour door open for the captain to pass out.

CHAPTER II. THE MONEY.

"THE stairs are very narrow, sir," said Alfred Raybrock to Captain Jorgan.

"Like my cabin-stairs," returned the captain, "on many a voyage."

"And they are rather inconvenient for the head."

"If my head can't take care of itself by this time, after all the knocking about the world it has had," replied the captain, as unconcernedly as if he had no connexion with it, "it's not worth looking after."

Thus, they came into the young fisherman's bedroom, which was as perfectly neat and clean as the shop and parlour below: though it was but a little place, with a sliding window, and a phrenological ceiling expressive of all the peculiarities of the house-roof. Here the captain sat down on the foot of the bed, and, glancing at a dreadful libel on Kitty which ornamented the wall—the production of some wandering limner, whom the captain secretly admired, as having studied portraiture from the figure-heads of ships—motioned to the young man to take the rush-chair on the other side of the small round table. That done, the captain put his hand into the deep breast-pocket of his long-skirted blue coat, and took out of it a strong square case-bottle—not a large bottle, but such as may be seen in any ordinary ship's medicine chest. Setting this bottle on the table without removing his hand from it, Captain Jorgan then spake as follows.

"In my last voyage homeward-bound," said the captain, "and that's the voyage off of which I now come straight, I encountered such weather off the Horn, as is not very often met with, even there. I have rounded that stormy Cape pretty often, and I believe I first beat about there in the identical storms that blew the devil's horns and tail off, and led to the horns being worked up into toothpicks for the plantation overseers in my country, who may be seen (if you travel down South, or away West, far enough) picking their teeth with 'em, while the whips, made of the tail, flog hard. In this last voyage, homeward-bound for Liverpool from South America, I tell you my young friend, it blew. Whole measures! No half measures, nor making believe to blow; it blew! Now, I warn't blown clean out of the water into the sky—though I expected to be even that—but I was blown clean out of my course; and when at last it fell calm, it fell dead calm, and a strong current set one way, day and night, night and day, and I drifted—drifted—drifted—out of all the ordinary tracks and courses of ships, and drifted yet, and yet drifted. It behoves a man who takes charge of fellow-critturs' lives, never to rest from making himself master of his calling. I never did rest, and consequently I knew pretty well ('specially looking over the side in the dead calm at that strong current), what dangers to expect, and what precautions to take against 'em. In short, we were driving head on, to an Island. There was no Island in the chart, and, therefore, you may say it was ill manners in the Island to be there; I don't dispute its bad breeding, but there it was. Thanks be to Heaven, I was as ready for the Island as the Island was ready for me. I made it out myself from the masthead, and I got enough way upon her in good time, to keep her off. I ordered a boat to be lowered and manned, and went in that boat myself to explore the Island. There was a reef outside it, and, floating in a corner of the smooth water within the reef, was a heap of seaweed, and entangled in that seaweed was this bottle."

Here, the captain took his hand from the

bottle for a moment, that the young fisherman might direct a wondering glance at it; and then replaced his hand and went on:

"If ever you come—or even if ever you don't come—to a desert place, use you your eyes and your spy-glass well; for the smallest thing you see, may prove of use to you, and may have some information or some warning in it. That's the principle on which I came to see this bottle. I picked up the bottle and ran the boat alongside the Island and made fast and went ashore, armed, with a part of my boat's crew. We found that every scrap of vegetation on the Island (I give it you as my opinion, but scant and scrubby at the best of times) had been consumed by fire. As we were making our way, cautiously and toilsomely, over the pulverised embers, one of my people sank into the earth, breast high. He turned pale, and 'Haul me out smart, shipmates,' says he, 'for my feet are among bones.' We soon got him on his legs again, and then we dug up the spot, and we found that the man was right, and that his feet had been among bones. More than that, they were human bones; though whether the remains of one man, or of two or three men, what with calcination and ashes, and what with a poor practical knowledge of anatomy, I can't undertake to say. We examined the whole Island and made out nothing else, save and except that, from its opposite side, I sighted a considerable tract of land, which land

I was able to identify, and according to the bearings of which (not to trouble you with my log) I took a fresh departure. When I got aboard again, I opened the bottle, which was oilskincovered as you see, and glass-stoppered as you see. Inside of it," pursued the captain, suiting his action to his words, "I found this little crumpled folded paper, just as you see. Outside of it was written, as you see, these words: '_Whoever finds this, is solemnly entreated by the dead, to convey it unread to Alfred Raybrock, Steepways, North Devon, England._' A sacred charge," said the captain, concluding his narrative, "and, Alfred Raybrock, there it is!"

"This is my poor brother's writing!"

"I supposed so," said Captain Jorgan. "I'll take a look out of this little window while you read it."

"Pray no, sir! I should be hurt. We should all be hurt. My brother couldn't know it would fall into such hands as yours."

The captain sat down again on the foot of the bed, and the young man opened the folded paper with a trembling hand, and spread it on the table. The ragged paper, evidently creased and torn both before and after being written on, was much blotted and stained, and the ink had faded and run, and many words were wanting. What the captain and the young fisherman made out together, after much re-reading and much humouring of the folds of the paper, was this:

The young fisherman had become more and more agitated, as the writing had become clearer to him. He now left it lying before the captain, over whose shoulder he had been reading it, and, dropping into his former seat, leaned forward on the table and laid his face in his hands.

"What, man," urged the captain, "don't give in! Be up and doing, like a man!"

"It is selfish, I know—but doing what, doing what?" cried the young fisherman, in complete despair, and stamping his sea-boot on the ground.

"Doing what?" returned the captain. "Something! I'd go down to the little break-water below, yonder, and take a wrench at one of the salt-rusted iron-rings there, and either wrench it up by the roots or wrench my teeth out of my head, sooner than I'd do nothing. Nothing!" ejaculated the captain. "Any fool or faint-heart can do that, and nothing can come of nothing—Which was pretended to be found out, I believe, by one of them Latin critturs," said the captain, with the deepest disdain; "as if Adam hadn't found it out, afore ever he so much as named the beasts!"

Yet the captain saw, in spite of his bold words, that there was some greater reason than he yet understood for the young man's distress. And he eyed him with a sympathising curiosity.

"Come, come!" continued the captain. "Speak out. What is it, boy?"

"You have seen how beautiful she is, sir," said the young man, looking up for the moment, with a flushed face and rumpled hair.

"Did any man ever say she warn't beautiful?" retorted the captain. "If so, go and lick him."

The young man laughed fretfully in spite of himself, and said, "It's not that, it's not that."

"Wa'al, then, what is it?" said the captain, in a more soothing tone.

The young fisherman mournfully composed himself to tell the captain what it was, and began: "We were to have been married next Monday week——"

"Were to have been!" interrupted Captain Jorgan. "And are to be? Hey?"

Young Raybrock shook his head, and traced out with his forefinger the words "poor father's five hundred pounds," in the written paper.

"Go along," said the captain. "Five hundred pounds? Yes?"

"That sum of money," pursued the young fisherman, entering with the greatest earnestness on his demonstration, while the captain eyed him with equal earnestness, "was all my late father possessed. When he died, he owed no man more than he left means to pay, but he had been able to lay by only five hundred pounds."

"Five hundred pounds," repeated the captain. "Yes?"

"In his lifetime, years before, he had expressly laid the money aside, to leave to my mother—like to settle upon her, if I make myself understood."

"Yes?"

"He had risked it once—my father put down in writing at that time, respecting the money—and was resolved never to risk it again."

"Not a spec'lator," said the captain. "My country wouldn't have suited him. Yes?"

"My mother has never touched the money till now. And now it was to have been laid out, this very next week, in buying me a handsome share in our neighbouring fishery here, to settle me in life with Kitty."

The captain's face fell, and he passed and repassed his sun-browned right hand over his thin hair, in a discomfited manner.

"Kitty's father has no more than enough to live on, even in the sparing way in which we live about here. He is a kind of bailiff or steward of manor rights here, and they are not much, and it is but a poor little office. He was better off once, and Kitty must never marry to mere drudgery and hard living."

The captain still sat stroking his thin hair, and looking at the young fisherman.

"I am as certain that my father had no knowledge that any one was wronged as to this money, or that any restitution ought to be made, as I am certain that the sun now shines. But, after this solemn warning from my brother's grave in the sea, that the money is Stolen Money," said Young Raybrock, forcing himself to the utterance of the words, "can I doubt it? Can I touch it?"

"About not doubting, I ain't so sure," observed the captain; "but about not touching—no—I don't think you can."

"See, then," said Young Raybrock, "why I am so grieved. Think of Kitty. Think what I have got to tell her!"

His heart quite failed him again when he had come round to that, and he once more beat his sea-boot softly on the floor. But, not for long; he soon began again, in a quietly resolute tone.

"However! Enough of that! You spoke some brave words to me just now, Captain Jorgan, and they shall not be spoken in vain. I have got to do Something. What I have got to do, before all other things, is to trace out the meaning of this paper, for the sake of the Good Name that has no one else to put it right or keep it right. And still, for the sake of the Good Name, and my father's memory, not a word of this writing must be breathed to my mother, or to Kitty, or to any human creature. You agree in this?"

"I don't know what they'll think of us, below," said the captain, "but for certain I can't oppose it. Now, as to tracing. How will you do?"

They both, as by consent, bent over the paper again, and again carefully puzzled out the whole of the writing.

"I make out that this would stand, if all the writing was here, 'Inquire among the old men living there, for'—some one. Most like, you'll go to this village named here?" said the captain, musing, with his finger on the name.

"Yes! And Mr. Tregarthen is a Cornishman, and—to be sure!—comes from Lanrean."

"Does he?" said the captain, quietly. "As I ain't acquainted with him, who may he be?"

"Mr. Tregarthen is Kitty's father."

"Ay, ay!" cried the captain. "Now, you speak! Tregarthen knows this village of Lanrean, then?"

"Beyond all doubt he does. I have often heard him mention it, as being his native place. He knows it well."

"Stop half a moment," said the captain. "We want a name here. You could ask Tregarthen (or if you couldn't, I could) what names of old men he remembers in his time in those diggings? Hey?"

"I can go straight to his cottage, and ask him now."

"Take me with you," said the captain, rising in a solid way that had a most comfortable reliability in it, "and just a word more, first. I have knocked about harder than you, and have got along further than you. I have had, all my sea-going life long, to keep my wits polished bright with acid and friction, like the brass cases of the ship's instruments. I'll keep you company on this expedition. Now, you don't live by talking, any more than I do. Clench that hand of yours in this hand of mine, and that's a speech on both sides."

Captain Jorgan took command of the expedition with that hearty shake. He at once refolded the paper exactly as before, replaced it in the bottle, put the stopper in, put the oilskin over the stopper, confided the whole to Young Raybrock's keeping, and led the way down stairs.

But it was harder navigation below stairs than above. The instant they set foot in the parlour, the quick womanly eye detected that there was something wrong. Kitty exclaimed, frightened, as she ran to her lover's side, "Alfred! What's the matter?" Mrs. Raybrock cried out to the captain, "Gracious! what have you done to my son to change him like this, all in a minute!" And the young widow—who was there with her work upon her arm—was at first so agitated, that she frightened the little girl she held in her hand, who hid her face in her mother's skirts and screamed. The captain, conscious of being held responsible for this domestic change, contemplated it with quite a guilty expression of countenance, and looked to the young fisherman to come to his rescue.

"Kitty darling," said Young Raybrock, "Kitty, dearest love, I must go away to Lanrean, and I don't know where else or how much farther, this very day. Worse than that—our marriage, Kitty, must be put off, and I don't know for how long."

Kitty stared at him, in doubt and wonder and in anger, and pushed him from her with her hand.

"Put off?" cried Mrs. Raybrock. "The marriage put off? And you going to Lanrean! Why, in the name of the dear Lord?"

"Mother dear, I can't say why, I must not

say why. It would be dishonourable and undutiful to say why."

"Dishonourable and undutiful?" returned the dame. "And is there nothing dishonourable or undutiful in the boy's breaking the heart of his own plighted love, and his mother's heart too, for the sake of the dark secrets and counsels of a wicked stranger? Why did you ever come here?" she apostrophised the innocent captain. "Who wanted you? Where did you come from? Why couldn't you rest in your own bad place, wherever it is, instead of disturbing the peace of quiet unoffending folk like us?"

"And what," sobbed the poor little Kitty, "have I ever done to you, you hard and cruel captain, that you should come and serve me so?"

And then they both began to weep most pitifully, while the captain could only look from the one to the other, and lay hold of himself by the coat-collar.

"Margaret," said the poor young fisherman, on his knees at Kitty's feet, while Kitty kept both her hands before her tearful face, to shut out the traitor from her view—but kept her fingers wide asunder and looked at him all the time: "Margaret, you have suffered so much, so uncomplainingly, and are always so careful and considerate! Do take my part, for poor Hugh's sake!"

The quiet Margaret was not appealed to in vain. "I will, Alfred," she returned, "and I do. I wish this gentleman had never come near us;" whereupon the captain laid hold of himself the tighter; "but I take your part, for all that. I am sure you have some strong reason and some sufficient reason for what you do, strange as it is, and even for not saying why you do it, strange as that is. And, Kitty darling, you are bound to think so, more than any one, for true love believes everything, and bears everything, and trusts everything. And mother dear, you are bound to think so too, for you know you have been blest with good sons, whose word was always as good as their oath, and who were brought up in as true a sense of honour as any gentlemen in this land. And I am sure you have no more call, mother, to doubt your living son than to doubt your dear son; and for the sake of the dear dead, I stand up for the dear living."

"Wa'al now," the captain struck in, with enthusiasm, "this I say. That whether your opinions flatter me or not, you are a young woman of sense and spirit and feeling; and I'd sooner have you by my side, in the hour of danger, than a good half of the men I've ever fallen in with—or fallen out with, ayther."

Margaret did not return the captain's compliment, or appear fully to reciprocate his good opinion, but she applied herself to the consolation of Kitty and of Kitty's mother-in-law that was to have been next Monday week, and soon restored the parlour to a quiet condition.

"Kitty, my darling," said the young fisherman, "I must go to your father to entreat him still to trust me in spite of this wretched change and mystery, and to ask him for some directions concerning Lanrean. Will you come home? Will you come with me, Kitty?"

Kitty answered not a word, but rose sobbing, with the end of her simple head-dress at her eyes. Captain Jorgan followed the lovers out, quite sheepishly: pausing in the shop to give an instruction to Mr. Pettifer.

"Here, Tom!" said the captain, in a low voice. "Here's something in your line. Here's an old lady poorly and low in her spirits. Cheer her up a bit, Tom. Cheer 'em all up."

Mr. Pettifer, with a brisk nod of intelligence, immediately assumed his steward face, and went with his quiet helpful steward step into the parlour: where the captain had the great satisfaction of seeing him, through the glass door, take the child in his arms (who offered no objection), and bend over Mrs. Raybrock, administering soft words of consolation.

"Though what he finds to say, unless he's telling her that it'll soon be over, or that most people is so at first, or that it'll do her good afterwards, I can not imaginate!" was the captain's reflection as he followed the lovers.

He had not far to follow them, since it was but a short descent down the stony ways to the cottage of Kitty's father. But, short as the distance was, it was long enough to enable the captain to observe that he was fast becoming the village Ogre; for, there was not a woman standing working at her door, or a fisherman coming up or going down, who saw Young Raybrock unhappy and little Kitty in tears, but she or he instantly darted a suspicious and indignant glance at the captain, as the foreigner who must somehow be responsible for this unusual spectacle. Consequently, when they came into Tregarthen's little garden—which formed the platform from which the captain had seen Kitty peeping over the wall—the captain brought to, and stood off and on at the gate, while Kitty hurried to hide her tears in her own room, and Alfred spoke with her father who was working in the garden. He was a rather infirm man, but could scarcely be called old yet, with an agreeable face and a promising air of making the best of things. The conversation began on his side with great cheerfulness and good humour, but soon became distrustful and soon angry. That was the captain's cue for striking both into the conversation and the garden.

"Morning, sir!" said Captain Jorgan. "How do you do?"

"The gentleman I am going away with," said the young fisherman to Tregarthen.

"Oh!" returned Kitty's father, surveying the unfortunate captain with a look of extreme disfavour. "I confess that I can't say I am glad to see you."

"No," said the captain, "and, to admit the truth, that seems to be the general opinion in these parts. But don't be hasty; you may think better of me, by-and-by."

"I hope so," observed Tregarthen.

"Wa'al, I hope so," observed the captain, quite at his ease; "more than that, I believe so —though you don't. Now, Mr. Tregarthen,

you don't want to exchange words of mistrust with me; and if you did, you couldn't, because I wouldn't. You and I are old enough to know better than to judge against experience from surfaces and appearances; and if you haven't lived to find out the evil and injustice of such judgments, you are a lucky man."

The other seemed to shrink under this remark, and replied, "Sir, I have lived to feel it deeply."

"Wa'al," said the captain, mollified, "then I've made a good cast, without knowing it. Now, Tregarthen, there stands the lover of your only child, and here stand I who know his secret. I warrant it a righteous secret, and none of his making, though bound to be of his keeping. I want to help him out with it, and tewwards that end we ask you to favour us with the names of two or three old residents in the village of Lanrean. As I am taking out my pocketbook and pencil to put the names down, I may as well observe to you that this, wrote atop of the first page here, is my name and address: 'Silas Jonas Jorgan, Salem, Massachusetts, United States.' If ever you take it in your head to run over, any morning, I shall be glad to welcome you. Now, what may be the spelling of these said names?"

"There was an elderly man," said Tregarthen, "named David Polreath. He may be dead."

"Wa'al," said the captain, cheerfully, "if Polreath's dead and buried, and can be made of any service to us, Polreath won't object to our digging of him up. Polreath's down, anyhow."

"There was another, named Penrewen. I don't know his Christian name."

"Never mind his Chris'en name," said the captain. "Penrewen for short."

"There was another, named John Tredgear."

"And a pleasant-sounding name, too," said the captain; "John Tredgear's booked."

"I can recal no other, except old Parvis."

"One of old Parvis's fam'ly, I reckon," said the captain, "kept a dry-goods store in New York city, and realised a handsome competency by burning his house to ashes. Same name, anyhow. David Polreath, Unchris'en Penrewen, John Tredgear, and old Arson Parvis."

"I cannot recal any others, at the moment."

"Thankee," said the captain. "And so, Tregarthen, hoping for your good opinion yet, and likewise for the fair Devonshire Flower's, your daughter's, I give you my hand, sir, and wish you good day."

Young Raybrock accompanied him disconsolately; for, there was no Kitty at the window when he looked up, no Kitty in the garden when he shut the gate, no Kitty gazing after them along the stony ways when they began to climb back.

"Now I tell you what," said the captain. "Not being at present calc'lated to promote harmony in your family, I won't come in. You go and get your dinner at home, and I'll get mine at the little hotel. Let our hour of meeting be two o'clock, and you'll find me smoking a cigar in the sun afore the hotel door. Tell Tom Pettifer, my steward, to consider himself on duty, and to look after your people till we come back; you'll find he'll have made himself useful to 'em already, and will be quite acceptable."

All was done as Captain Jorgan directed. Punctually at two o'clock, the young fisherman appeared with his knapsack at his back; and punctually at two o'clock, the captain jerked away the last feathery end of his cigar.

"Let me carry your baggage, Captain Jorgan; I can easily take it with mine."

"Thank'ee," said the captain, "I'll carry it myself. It's on'y a comb."

They climbed out of the village, and paused among the trees and fern on the summit of the hill above, to take breath and to look down at the beautiful sea. Suddenly, the captain gave his leg a resounding slap, and cried, "Never knew such a right thing in all my life!"—and ran away.

The cause of this abrupt retirement on the part of the captain, was little Kitty among the trees. The captain went out of sight and waited, and kept out of sight and waited, until it occurred to him to beguile the time with another cigar. He lighted it, and smoked it out, and still he was out of sight and waiting. He stole within sight at last, and saw the lovers, with their arms entwined and their bent heads touching, moving slowly among the trees. It was the golden time of the afternoon then, and the captain said to himself, "Golden sun, golden sea, golden sails, golden leaves, golden love, golden youth—a golden state of things altogether!"

Nevertheless, the captain found it necessary to hail his young companion before going out of sight again. In a few moments more, he came up, and they began their journey.

"That still young woman with the fatherless child," said Captain Jorgan as they fell into step, "didn't throw her words away; but good honest words are never thrown away. And now that I am conveying you off from that tender little thing that loves and relies and hopes, I feel just as if I was the snarling crittur in the picters, with the tight legs, the long nose, and the feather in his cap, the tips of whose mustachios get up nearer to his eyes, the wickeder he gets."

The young fisherman knew nothing of Mephistopheles; but, he smiled when the captain stopped to double himself up and slap his leg, and they went along in right good fellowship.

CHAPTER III. THE CLUB-NIGHT.

A CORNISH MOOR, when the east wind drives over it, is as cold and rugged a scene as a traveller is likely to find in a year's travel. A Cornish Moor in the dark, is as black a solitude as the traveller is likely to wish himself well out of, in the course of a life's wanderings. A Cornish Moor in a night fog, is a wilderness where the traveller needs to know his way well, or the chances are very strong that his life and his wanderings will soon perplex him no more.

Captain Jorgan and the young fisherman had faced the east and the south-east winds, from the first rising of the sun after their departure from the village of Steepways. Thrice, had the sun risen, and still all day long had the sharp wind blown at them like some malevolent spirit bent on forcing them back. But, Captain Jorgan was too familiar with all the winds that blow, and too much accustomed to circumvent their slightest weaknesses and get the better of them in the long run, to be beaten by any member of the airy family. Taking the year round, it was his opinion that it mattered little what wind blew, or how hard it blew; so, he was as indifferent to the wind on this occasion as a man could be who frequently observed "that it freshened him up," and who regarded it in the light of an old acquaintance. One might have supposed from his way, that there was even a kind of fraternal understanding between Captain Jorgan and the wind, as between two professed fighters often opposed to one another. The young fisherman, for his part, was accustomed within his narrower limits to hold hard weather cheap, and had his anxious object before him; so, the wind went by him too, little heeded, and went upon its way to kiss Kitty.

Their varied course had lain by the side of the sea where the brown rocks cleft it into fountains of spray, and inland where once barren moors were reclaimed and cultivated, and by lonely villages of poor-enough cabins with mud walls, and by a town or two with an old church and a market-place. But, always travelling through a sparely inhabited country and over a broad expanse, they had come at last upon the true Cornish Moor within reach of Lanrean. None but gaunt spectres of miners passed them here, with metallic masks of faces, ghastly with dust of copper and tin; anon, solitary works on remote hill-tops, and bare machinery of torturing wheels and cogs and chains, writhing up hill-sides, were the few scattered hints of human presence in the landscape; during long intervals, the bitter wind, howling and tearing at them like a fierce wild monster, had them all to itself.

"A sing'lar thing it is," said the captain, looking round at the brown desert of rank grass and poor moss, "how like this airth is, to the men that live upon it! Here's a spot of country rich with hidden metals, and it puts on the worst rags of clothes possible, and crouches and shivers and makes believe to be so poor that it can't so much as afford a feed for a beast. Just like a human miser, ain't it?"

"But they find the miser out," returned the young fisherman, pointing to where the earth by the watercourses and along the valleys was turned up, for miles, in trying for metal.

"Ay, they find him out," said the captain; "but he makes a struggle of it even then, and holds back all he can. He's a 'cute 'un."

The gloom of evening was already gathering on the dreary scene, and they were, at the shortest and best, a dozen miles from their destination. But, the captain, in his long-skirted blue coat and his boots and his hat and his square shirt-collar, and without any extra defence against the weather, walked coolly along with his hands in his pockets : as if he lived underground somewhere hard by, and had just come up to show his friend the road.

"I'd have liked to have had a look at this place, too," said the captain, "when there was a monstrous sweep of water rolling over it, dragging the powerful great stones along and piling 'em atop of one another, and depositing the foundations for all manner of superstitions. Bless you ! the old priests, smart mechanical critturs as they were, never piled up many of these stones. Water's the lever that moved 'em. When you see 'em thick and blunt tewwards one point of the compass, and fined away thin tewwards the opposite point, you may be as good as moral sure that the name of the ancient Druid that fixed 'em was Water."

The captain referred to some great blocks of stone presenting this characteristic, which were wonderfully balanced and heaped on one another, on a desolate hill. Looking back at these, as they stood out against the lurid glare of the west, just then expiring, they were not unlike enormous antediluvian birds, that had perched there on crags and peaks, and had been petrified there.

"But it's an interesting country," said the captain, " —fact ! It's old in the annals of that said old Arch Druid, Water, and it's old in the annals of the said old parson-critturs too. It's a mighty interesting thing to set your boot (as I did this day) on a rough honeycombed old stone, with just nothing you can name but weather visible upon it: which the scholars that go about with hammers, chipping pieces off the universal airth, find to be an inscription, entreating prayers for the soul of some for-ages-bust-up crittur of a governor that over-taxed a people never heard of." Here the captain stopped to slap his leg. "It's a mighty interesting thing to come upon a score or two of stones set up on end in a desert, some short, some tall, some leaning here, some leaning there, and to know that they were pop'larly supposed —and may be still—to be a group of Cornish men that got changed into that geological formation for playing a game upon a Sunday. They wouldn't have it in my country, I reckon, even if they could get it—but it's very interesting."

In this, the captain, though it amused him, was quite sincere. Quite as sincere as when he added, after looking well about him : "That fog-bank coming up as the sun goes down, will spread, and we shall have to feel our way into Lanreau full as much as see it."

All the way along, the young fisherman had spoken at times to the captain, of his interrupted hopes, and of the family good name, and of the restitution that must be made, and of the cherished plans of his heart so near attainment, which must be set aside for it. In his simple faith and honour, he seemed incapable of entertaining the idea that it was within the bounds of possibility to evade the doing of what their

inquiries should establish to be right. This was very agreeable to Captain Jorgan, and won his genuine admiration. Wherefore, he now turned the discourse back into that channel, and encouraged his companion to talk of Kitty, and to calculate how many years it would take, without a share in the fishery, to establish a home for her, and to relieve his honest heart by dwelling on its anxieties.

Meanwhile, it fell very dark, and the fog became dense, though the wind howled at them and hit them as savagely as ever. The captain had carefully taken the bearings of Lanrean from the map, and carried his pocket compass with him : the young fisherman, too, possessed that kind of cultivated instinct for shaping a course, which is often found among men of such pursuits. But, although they held a true course in the main, and corrected it when they lost the road by the aid of the compass and a light obtained with great difficulty in the roomy depths of the captain's hat, they could not help losing the road often. On such occasions they would become involved in the difficult ground of the spongy moor, and, after making a laborious loop, would emerge upon the road at some point they had passed before they left it, and thus would have a good deal of work to do twice over. But the young fisherman was not easily lost, and the captain (and his comb) would probably have turned up, with perfect coolness and self-possession, at any appointed spot on the surface of this globe. Consequently, they were no more than retarded in their progress to Lanrean, and arrived in that small place at nine o'clock. By that time, the captain's hat had fallen back over his ears and rested on the nape of his neck ; but he still had his hands in his pockets, and showed no other sign of dilapidation.

They had almost run against a low stone house with red-curtained windows, before they knew they had hit upon the little hotel, the King Arthur's Arms. They could just descry through the mist, on the opposite side of the narrow road, other low stone buildings which were its outhouses and stables ; and somewhere overhead, its invisible sign was being wrathfully swung by the wind.

"Now, wait a bit," said the captain. "They might be full here, or they might offer us cold quarters. Consequently, the policy is to take an observation, and, when we've found the warmest room, walk right slap into it."

The warmest room was evidently that from which fire and candle streamed reddest and brightest, and from which the sound of voices engaged in some discussion came out into the night. Captain Jorgan having established the bearings of this room, merely said to his young friend, " Follow me !" and was in it, before King Arthur's Arms had any notion that they enfolded a stranger.

"Order, order, order !" cried several voices, as the captain with his hat under his arm, stood within the door he had opened.

"Gentlemen," said the captain, advancing, "I am much beholden to you for the opportunity you give me of addressing you; but will not detain you with any lengthened observations. I have the honour to be a cousin of yours on the Uncle Sam side; this young friend of mine is a nearer relation of yours on the Devonshire side; we are both pretty nigh used up, and much in want of supper. I thank you for your welcome, and I am proud to take you by the hand, sir, and I hope I see you well."

These last words were addressed to a jolly looking chairman with a wooden hammer near him: which, but for the captain's friendly grasp, he would have taken up, and hammered the table with.

"How do you *do*, sir?" said the captain, shaking this chairman's hand with the greatest heartiness, while his new friend ineffectually eyed his hammer of office; "when you come to my country, I shall be proud to return your welcome, sir, and that of this good company."

The captain now took his seat near the fire, and invited his companion to do the like—whom he congratulated aloud, on their having "fallen on their feet."

The company, who might be about a dozen in number, were at a loss what to make of, or do with, the captain. But, one little old man in long flapping shirt collars: who, with only his face and them visible through a cloud of tobacco smoke, looked like a superannuated Cherubim: said sharply,

"This is a Club."

"This is a Club," the captain repeated to his young friend. "Wa'al now, that's curious! Didn't I say, coming along, if we could only light upon a Club?"

The captain's doubling himself up and slapping his leg, finished the chairman. He had been softening towards the captain from the first, and he melted. "Gentlemen King Arthurs," said he, rising, "though it is not the custom to admit strangers, still, as we have broken the rule once to-night, I will exert my authority and break it again. And while the supper of these travellers is cooking;" here his eye fell on the landlord, who discreetly took the hint and withdrew to see about it; "I will recal you to the subject of the seafaring man."

"D'ye hear!" said the captain, aside to the young fisherman; "that's in our way. Who's the seafaring man, I wonder?"

"I see several old men here," returned the young fisherman, eagerly, for his thoughts were always on his object. "Perhaps one or more of the old men whose names you wrote down in your book, may be here."

"Perhaps," said the captain; "I've got my eye on 'em. But don't force it. Try if it won't come nat'ral."

Thus the two, behind their hands, while they sat warming them at the fire. Simultaneously, the Club beginning to be at its ease again, and resuming the discussion of the seafaring man, the captain winked to his fellow-traveller to let him attend to it.

As it was a kind of conversation not altogether unprecedented in such assemblages, where

most of those who spoke at all, spoke all at once, and where half of those could put no beginning to what they had to say, and the other half could put no end, the tendency of the debate was discursive, and not very intelligible. All the captain had made out, down to the time when the separate little table laid for two was covered with a smoking broiled fowl and rashers of bacon, reduced itself to these words. That, a seafaring man had arrived at The King Arthur's Arms, benighted, an hour or so earlier in the evening. That, the Gentlemen King Arthurs had admitted him, though all unknown, into the sanctuary of their Club. That, they had invited him to make his footing good by telling a story. That, he had, after some pressing, begun a story of adventure and shipwreck: at an interesting point of which he suddenly broke off, and positively refused to finish. That, he had been thereupon taken up a candlestick, and gone to bed, and was now the sole occupant of a double-bedded room up-stairs. The question raised on these premises, appeared to be, whether the seafaring man was not in a state of contumacy and contempt, and ought not to be formally voted and declared in that condition. This deliberation involved the difficulty (suggested by the more jocose and irreverent of the Gentlemen King Arthurs) that it might make no sort of difference to the seafaring man whether he was so voted and declared, or not.

Captain Jorgan and the young fisherman ate their supper and drank their beer, and their knives and forks had ceased to rattle and their glasses had ceased to clink, and still the discussion showed no symptoms of coming to any conclusion. But, when they had left their little supper-table and had returned to their seats by the fire, the Chairman hammered himself into attention, and thus outspake.

"Gentlemen King Arthurs; when the night is so bad without, harmony should prevail within. When the moor is so windy, cold, and bleak, this room should be cheerful, convivial, and entertaining. Gentlemen, at present it is neither the one, nor yet the other, nor yet the other. Gentlemen King Arthurs, I recal you to yourselves. Gentlemen King Arthurs, what are you? You are inhabitants—old inhabitants—of the noble village of Lanrean. You are in council assembled. You are a monthly Club through all the winter months, and they are many. It is your perroud perrivilege, on a new member's entrance, or on a member's birthday, to call upon that member to make good his footing by relating to you some transaction or adventure in his life, or in the life of a relation, or in the life of a friend, and then to depute me as your representative to spin a teetotum to pass it round. Gentlemen King Arthurs, your perroud perrivileges shall not suffer in my keeping. N—no! Therefore, as the member whose birthday the present occasion has the honour to be, has gratified you; and as the seafaring man overhead has *not* gratified you; I start you fresh, by spinning the teetotum attached to my office, and calling on the gentleman it falls to, to speak up when his name is declared."

The captain and his young friend looked hard at the teetotum as it whirled rapidly, and harder still when it gradually became intoxicated and began to stagger about the table in an ill-conducted and disorderly manner. Finally, it came into collision with a candlestick and leaped against the pipe of the old gentleman with the flapping shirt collars. Thereupon, the chairman struck the table once with his hammer and said :

"Mr. Parvis!"

"D'ye hear that?" whispered the captain, greatly excited, to the young fisherman. "I'd have laid you a thousand dollars a good half-hour ago, that that old cherubim in the clouds was Arson Parvis!"

The respectable personage in question, after turning up one eye to assist his memory—at which time, he bore a very striking resemblance indeed to the conventional representations of his race as executed in oil by various ancient masters—commenced a narrative, of which the interest centred in a waistcoat. It appeared that the waistcoat was a yellow waistcoat with a green stripe, white sleeves, and a plain brass button. It also appeared that the waistcoat was made to order, by Nicholas Pendold of Penzance, who was thrown off the top of a four-horse coach coming down the hill on the Plymouth road, and, pitching on his head where he was not sensitive, lived two-and-thirty years afterwards, and considered himself the better for the accident—roused up, as it might be. It further appeared that the waistcoat belonged to Mr. Parvis's father, and had once attended him, in company with a pair of gaiters, to the annual feast of miners at St. Just : where the extraordinary circumstance which ever afterwards rendered it a waistcoat famous in story had occurred. But, the celebrity of the waistcoat was not thoroughly accounted for by Mr. Parvis, and had to be to some extent taken on trust by the company, in consequence of that gentleman's entirely forgetting all about the extraordinary circumstance that had handed it down to fame. Indeed, he was even unable, on a gentle cross-examination instituted for the assistance of his memory, to inform the Gentlemen King Arthurs whether it was a circumstance of a natural or supernatural character. Having thus responded to the teetotum, Mr. Parvis, after looking out from his clouds as if he would like to see the man who would beat that, subsided into himself.

The fraternity were plunged into a blank condition by Mr. Parvis's success, and the chairman was about to try another spin, when young Raybrock—whom Captain Jorgan had with difficulty restrained—rose, and said might he ask Mr. Parvis a question

The Gentlemen King Arthurs holding, with loud cries of "Order!" that he might not, he asked the question as soon as he could possibly make himself heard.

Did the forgotten circumstance relate in any way to money? To a sum of money, such as five hundred pounds? To money supposed by its possessor to be honestly come by, but in reality ill-gotten and stolen?

A general surprise seized upon the club when this remarkable inquiry was preferred ; which would have become resentment but for the captain's interposition.

"Strange as it sounds," said he, "and suspicious as it sounds, I pledge myself, gentlemen, that my young friend here has a manly stand-up Cornish reason for his words. Also, I pledge myself that they are inoffensive words. He and I are searching for information on a subject which those words generally describe. Such information we may get from the honestest and best of men—may get, or not get, here or anywhere about here. I hope the Honourable Mr. Arson—I ask his pardon—Parvis—will not object to quiet my young friend's mind by saying Yes or No.

After some time, the obtuse Mr. Parvis was with great trouble and difficulty induced to roar out "No!" For which concession the captain rose and thanked him.

"Now, listen to the next," whispered the captain to the young fisherman. "There may be more in him than in the other crittur. Don't interrupt him. Hear him out."

The chairman with all due formality spun the teetotum, and it reeled into the brandy-and-water of a strong brown man of sixty or so : John Tredgear : the manager of a neighbouring mine. He immediately began as follows, with a plain business-like air that gradually warmed as he proceeded.

It happened that at one period of my life the path of my destiny (not a tin path then) lay along the highways and byways of France, and that I had occasion to make frequent stoppages at common French roadside cabarets—that kind of tavern which has a very bad name in French books and French plays. I had engaged myself in an undertaking which rendered such journeys necessary. A very old friend of mine had recently established himself at Paris in a wholesale commercial enterprise, into the nature of which it is not necessary for our present purpose to enter. He had proposed to me a certain share in the undertaking, and one of the duties of my post was to involve occasional journeys among the smaller towns and villages of France, with the view of establishing agencies and opening connexions. My friend had applied to me to undertake this function, rather than to a native, feeling that he could trust me better than a stranger. He knew also that, in consequence of my having been half my life at school in France, my knowledge of the language would be sufficient for every purpose that could be required.

I accepted my friend's proposal, and entered with such energy as I could command upon my new mode of life. Sometimes, my journeyings from place to place were accomplished by means of the railroad, or other public conveyance; but there were other occasions, and these last I liked the best, when it was necessary I should go to out-of-the-way places, and by such cross-roads as rendered it more convenient for me to travel with a carriage and horse of my own. My carriage was a kind of phaeton without a coach-box, with a leather hood that would put up and down; and there was plenty of room at the back, for such specimens or samples of goods as it was necessary that I should carry with me. For my horse—it was absolutely indispensable that it should be an animal of some value, as no horse but a very good one would be capable of performing the long courses day after day which my mode of travelling rendered necessary. He cost me two thousand francs, and was anything but dear at the price.

Many were the journeys we performed together over the broad acres of beautiful France. Many were the hotels, many the auberges, many the bad dinners, many the damp beds, and many the fleas which I encountered en route. Many were the dull old fortified towns over whose drawbridges I rolled; many the still more dull old towns without fortifications and without drawbridges, at which my avocations made it necessary for me to halt.

I don't know how it was that on the morning when I was to start from the town of Doulaise, with the intention of sleeping at Francy-le-Grand, I was an hour later in commencing my journey than I ought to have been. I have said I don't know how it was, but this is scarcely true. I do know how it was. It was because on that morning, to use a popular expression, everything went wrong. So, it was an hour later than it ought to have been, gentlemen, when I drew up the sheepskin lining of my carriage apron over my legs, and establishing my little dog comfortably on the seat beside me, set off on my journey. In all my expeditions I was accompanied by a favourite terrier of mine, which I had brought with me from England. I never travelled without her, and found her a companion.

It was a miserable day in the month of October. A perfectly grey sky, with white gleams about the horizon, gave unmistakable evidence that the small drizzle which was falling would continue for four-and-twenty hours at least. It was cold and cheerless weather, and on the deserted road I was pursuing, there was scarcely a human being (unless it was an occasional cantonnier, or road-mender) to break the solitude. A deserted way indeed, with poplars on each side of it, which had turned yellow in the autumn, and had shed their leaves in abundance all across the road, so that my mare's footsteps had quite a muffled sound as she trampled them under her hoofs. Widely-extending flats spread out on either side till the view was lost in an inconceivably melancholy scene, and the road itself was so perfectly straight, that you could see something like ten miles of it diminishing to a point in front of you, while a similar view was visible through the little window at the back of the carriage.

In the hurry of the morning's departure I had omitted to inquire, as I generally did in travelling an unknown road, at what village it would be best for me to stop, about noon, to bait, and what was the name of the most respectable house of public entertainment in my way; so that when I arrived between twelve and one o'clock at a certain place where four roads met; and when at one of the corners formed by their union I saw a great bare-looking inn, with the sign of the Tête Noire swinging in front; I had nothing for it but to put up there, without knowing anything of the character of the house.

The look of the place did not please me. It was a great bare uninhabited-looking house, which seemed much larger than was necessary, and presented a black and dirty appearance, which, considering the distance from any town, it was difficult to account for. All the doors and all the windows were shut; there was no sign of any living creature about the place; and niched into the wall above the principal entrance was a grim and ghastly-looking life-size figure of a Saint. For a moment I hesitated whether I should turn into the open gates of the stable-yard, or go further in search of some more attractive halting-place. But my mare was tired, I was more than half way on my road, and this would be the best division of the journey. Besides, Gentlemen; why not put up here? If I was only going to stop at such places of entertainment as completely satisfied me, externally as well as internally, I had better give up travelling altogether.

There were no more signs of life in the interior of the yard, than were presented by the external aspect of the house, as it fronted the road. Everything seemed shut up. All the stables and outhouses were characterised by closed doors, without so much as a straw clinging to their thresholds to indicate that these buildings were sometimes put to a practical use. I saw no manure strewed about the place, and no living creature: no pigs, no ducks, no fowls. It was perfectly still and quiet, and, as it was one of those days when a fine small rain descends quite straight, without a breath of air to drive it one way or other, the silence was complete and distressing. I gave a loud shout, and began undoing the harness while my summons was taking effect.

The first person whom the sound of my voice appeared to have reached, was a small but precocious boy: who opened a door in the back of the house, and, descending the flight of steps which led to it, approached to aid me in my task. I was just undoing the final buckle on my side of the harness, when, happening to turn round, I discovered, standing close behind me, a personage who had approached so quietly that it would have been a confusing thing to find him so near even if there had been nothing in his appearance which was calculated to startle one. He was the most ill-looking man, Gentlemen, that it was ever my fortune to behold. Nearer fifty than any other age I could give him, his dry spare nature had kept him as light and active as a restless boy. An absence of flesh, however, was not the only want I felt to exist in the personal appearance of the landlord of the Tête Noire. There was a much more serious defect in him than this. A want of any hint of mercy, or conscience, or any accessible approach to the better side (if there was a better side) of the man's nature. When first I looked at his eyes, as he stood behind me in the open court, and as they rapidly glanced over the comely points of my horse, and thence to the packages inside my carriage and the portmanteau strapped on in front of it—at that time, the colour of his eyes appeared to me to be of an almost orange tinge; but when, a minute afterwards, we stood together in the dark stable, I noted that a kind of blue phosphorescence gleamed upon their surface, veiling their real hue, and imparting to them a tigerish lustre. The moment when I remarked this, by-the-by, was when the organs I have been describing were fixed upon the very large gold ring which I had not ceased to wear when I adopted my adventurous life, and which you may see upon my finger now. There were two other things about this man that struck me. These were, a bald red projecting lump of flesh at the back of his head, and a deep scar, which a scrap of frouzy whisker on his cheek wholly declined to conceal.

"A nasty day for a journey of pleasure," said the landlord, looking at me with a satirical smile.

"Perhaps it is *not* a journey of pleasure," I answered, dryly.

"We have few such travellers on the road now," said the evil-faced man. "The railroads make the country a desert, and the roads are as wild as they were three hundred years ago."

"They are well enough," I answered, carelessly, "for those who are obliged to travel by them. Nobody else, I should think, would be likely to make use of them."

"Will you come into the house?" said the landlord, abruptly, looking me full in the face.

I never felt a stronger repugnance than I entertained towards the idea of entering this man's doors. Yet what other course was open to me. My mare was already half through the first instalment of her oats, so there was no more excuse for remaining in the stable. To take a walk in the drenching rain was out of the question, and to remain sitting in my calèche would have been a worse indication of suspicion and mistrust. Besides, I had had nothing since the morning's coffee, and I wanted something to eat and drink. There was nothing to be done, then, but to accept my ill-looking friend's offer. He led the way up the flight of steps which gave access to the interior of the building.

The room in which I found myself on passing through the door at the top of these steps, was one of those rooms which an excess of light not only fails to enliven, but seems even to invest with an additional degree of gloom. There is *sometimes* this character about light, and

I have seen before now, a workhouse ward, and a barren schoolroom, which have owed a good share of their melancholy to an immoderate amount of cold grey daylight. This room, then, into which I was shown, was one of those which, on a wet day, seemed several degrees lighter than the open air. Of course it could not be really lighter than the thing that lit it, but it seemed so. It also appeared larger than the whole out-door world; and this, certainly, could not be either, but seemed so. Vast as it was, there appeared through two glass-doors in one of the walls another apartment of similar dimensions. It was not a square room, nor an oblong room, but was smaller at one end than at the other : a phenomenon which, as you have very likely observed, Gentlemen, has always an unpleasant effect. The billiard-table, which stood in the middle of the apartment, though really of the usual size, looked quite a trifling piece of furniture; and as to the other tables, which were planted sparingly here and there for purposes of refreshment, they were quite lost in the immensity of space about them. A cupboard, a rack of billiard cues, a marking-board, and a print of the murder of the Archbishop of Paris in a black frame, alone broke the uniformity of wall. The ceiling, as far as one could judge of anything at that altitude, appeared to be traversed by an enormous beam with rings fastened into it adapted for suicidal purposes, and splashed with the whitewash with which the ceiling itself and the walls had just been decorated. Even my little terrier, whom I had been obliged to take up in my arms on account of the disposition she had manifested to fly at the shins of our detested landlord, looked round the room with a gaze of horror as I set her down, and trembled and shivered as if she would come out of her skin.

"And so you don't like him, Nelly, and your little beads of eyes, that look up at me from under that hairy penthouse, with nothing but love in them, are all a-blaze with fury when they are turned upon his sinister face? And how did he get that scar, Nelly? Did he get it when he slaughtered his last traveller? And what do you think of his eyes, Nelly? And what do you think of the back of his head, my dog? What do you think he's about now, eh? What mischief do you think he's hatching? Don't you wish you were sitting by my side in the calèche, and that we were out on the free road again?"

To all these questions and remarks, my little companion responded very intelligibly by faint thumpings of the ground with her tail, and by certain flutterings of her ears, which, from long habits of intercourse, I understood very well to mean that whatever my opinion might be, she coincided in it.

I had ordered an omelette and some wine when I first entered the house, and, as I now sat waiting for it, I observed that my landlord would every now and then leave what he was about in the other room—where I concluded that he was engaged preparing my meal—and would come and peer at me furtively through the glass-doors which connected the room I was in, with that in which he was. Once, too, I heard him go out, and I felt sure that he had retired to the stables, to examine more minutely the value of my horse and carriage.

I took it into my head that my landlord was a desperate rogue; that his business was not sufficient to support him; that he had remarked that I was in possession of a very valuable horse, a carriage which would fetch something, and a quantity of luggage in which there were probably articles of price. I had other things of worth about my person, including a sum of money, without which I could not be travelling about, as he saw me, from place to place.

While my mind was amusing itself with these cheerful reflections, a little girl, of about twelve years old, entered the room through the glass-doors, and, after honouring me with a long stare, went to the cupboard at the other end of the apartment, and, opening it with a bunch of keys which she brought with her in her hand, took out a small white paper packet, about four inches square, and retired with it by the way by which she had entered; still staring at me so diligently that, from want of proper attention to where she was going, she got (I am happy to state) a severe bump against the door as she passed through it. She was a horrid little girl this, with eyes that in shirking the necessity of looking straight at anybody or anything, had got at last to look only at her nose—finding it, probably, as bad a nose as could be met with, and therefore a congenial companion. She had, moreover, frizzy and fluey hair, was excessively dirty, and had a slow crab-like way of going along without looking at what she was about, which was very noisome and detestable.

It was not long before this young lady reappeared, bearing in her hand a plate containing the omelette, which she placed upon the table without going through the previous form of laying a cloth. She next cut an immense piece of bread from a loaf shaped like a ring, and, having clapped this also down upon the dirtiest part of the table, and having further favoured me with a wiped knife and fork, disappeared once more. She disappeared to fetch the wine. When this had been brought, and some water, the preparations for my feast were considered complete, and I was left to enjoy it alone.

I must not omit to mention that the horrid waiting-maid appeared to excite as strong an antipathy in the breast of my little dog as that which my landlord himself had stirred up; and, I am happy to say, that as the child left the room I was obliged to interfere, to prevent Nelly from harassing her retreating calves.

Gentlemen, an experienced traveller soon learns that he must eat to support nature: closing his eyes, nose, and ears to all suggestions. I set to work, then, at the omelette with energy, and at the tough sour bread with good will, and had swallowed half a tumbler of wine and water, when a thought suddenly occurred to me which caused me to set the glass down upon the table. I had no sooner done this, than I raised it again to my lips, took a fresh sip, rolled the liquid about in my mouth two or three times, and spat it out upon the floor. But I uttered, as I did so, in an audible tone, the monosyllable "Pooh!"

"Pooh! Nelly," I said, looking down at my dog, who was watching me intensely with her head on one side—"pooh! Nelly," I repeated, "what frantic and inconceivable nonsense!"

And what was it that I thus stigmatised? What was it that had given me pause in the middle of my draught? What thought was it that caused me to set down my glass with half its contents remaining in it? It was a suspicion, driven straight and swift as an arrow into the innermost recesses of my soul, that the wine I had just been drinking, and which, contrary to my custom, I had mingled with water, was drugged!

There are some thoughts which, like noxious insects, come buzzing back into one's mind as often as we repulse them. We confute them in argument, prove them illogical, leave them not a leg to stand upon, and yet there they are the next moment as brisk as bees, and stronger on their pins than ever. It was just such a thought as this with which I had now to deal. It was well to say "Pooh!" it was well to remind myself that this was the nineteenth century, that I was not acting a part in a French melodrama, that such things as I was thinking of were only known in romances; it was well to argue that to set a respectable man down as a murderer, because he had peculiar coloured eyes and a scar upon his cheek; were ridiculous things to do. There seemed to be two separate parties within me: one possessed of great powers of argument and a cool judgment: the other, an irrational or opposition party, whose chief force consisted in a system of dogged assertion, which all the arguments of the rational party were insufficient to put down.

It was not long before an additional force was imparted to the tactics of the irrational party, by certain symptoms which began to develop themselves in my internal organisation, and which seemed favourable to the view of the case I was so anxious to refute. In spite of all my efforts to the contrary, I could not help feeling that some very remarkable sensations were slowly and gradually stealing over me. First of all, I began to find that I was a little at fault in my system of calculating distances: so that when I took up any object and attempted to replace it on the table, I either brought it into contact with that article of furniture with a crash, in consequence of conceiving it to be lower than it was; or else, imagining that the table was several inches nearer to the ceiling than was the case, I abandoned whatever I held in my hand sooner than I should, and found that I was confiding it to space. Then, again, my head felt light upon my shoulders, there was a slight tingling in my hands, and a sense that they, as well as my feet (which were very cold), were swelling to gigantic size, and were also surrounded with numerous rapidly revolving wheels of a light structure, like Catherine-wheels previous to ignition. It also appeared to me that when I spoke to my dog, my voice had a curious sound, and my words were very imperfectly articulated.

It would happen, too, that when I looked towards the glass-doors, my landlord was there, peering at me through the muslin curtains : or the horrid little girl would enter, with no obvious intention, and having loitered for a little time about the room, would leave it again. At length the landlord himself came in, and coolly walking up to the table at which I was seated, glanced at the hardly tasted wine before me.

"It would appear that the wine of the country is not to your taste," he said.

"It is good enough," I answered, as carelessly as I could ; the words sounding to me as if they were uttered inside the cupola of St. Paul's, and were conveyed by iron tubes to the place I occupied.

I was in a strange state—perfectly conscious, but imperfectly able to control my thoughts, my words, my actions. I believe my landlord stood staring down at me as I sat staring up at him, and watching the Catherine-wheels as they revolved round his eyes and nose and chin—Gentlemen, they seemed absolutely to *fizz* when they got to the scar on his cheek.

At this time a noisy party entered the main room of the auberge, which I have described as being visible through the glass-doors, and the landlord had to leave me for a time, to go and attend to them. I think I must have fallen into a slight and strongly-resisted doze, and that when I started out of it, it was in consequence of the violent barking of my terrier. The landlord was in the room ; he was just unlocking the cupboard from which the little girl had taken the paper parcel. He took out just such another paper parcel, and returned again through the doors. As he did so, I remember stupidly wondering what had become of the little girl. Presently his evil face appeared again at the door.

"I am going to prepare the coffee," said the landlord ; "perhaps monsieur will like it better than the wine."

As the man disappeared, I started suddenly and violently upon my feet. I could deceive myself no longer. My thoughts were like lightning. "The wine having been taken in so small a quantity and so profusely mixed with water, has done its work (as this man can see) but imperfectly. The coffee will finish that work. He is now preparing it. The cupboard, the little parcel—there can be no doubt. I will leave this place while I yet can. Now or never ; if those men whose voices I hear in the other room leave the house it will be too late. With so many witnesses, no attempt can be made to prevent my departure. I *will* not sleep—I *will* act—I *will* force my muscles to their work, and get away from this place."

Gentlemen ; in compensation for a set of nerves of distressing sensitiveness, I have received from nature a remarkable power of controlling my nerves for a time. I staggered to the door, closing it after me more violently than I had intended, and descended—the fresh air making me feel very giddy—into the yard.

As I went down the steps, I saw the truculent little girl of whom I have already spoken entering the yard, followed by a blacksmith, carrying a hammer and some other implements of his trade. Catching sight of me, the little girl spoke quickly to the blacksmith, and in an instant they both changed their course, which was directed towards the stable, and entered an outhouse on the other side of the yard. The thought entered my head that this man had been sent for to drive a nail into my horse's foot, so that in the event of the drugged wine failing I might still be unable to proceed. This horrible idea added new force to my exertions. I seized the shafts of my carriage and commenced dragging it out of the yard and round to the front of the house : feeling that if it was once in the highway, there would be less possibility of offering any impediment to my starting. I am conscious of having fallen twice to the ground, in my struggles to get the carriage out of the yard. Next, I hastened to the stable. My mare was still harnessed, with the exception of the head-stall. I managed to get the bit into her mouth, and dragged her to the place where I had left the carriage. After I know not how many efforts to place the docile beast in the shafts—for I was as incapable of calculating distances as a drunken man—I recollect, but how I know not, securing the assistance of the boy I had seen. I was making a final effort to fasten the trace to its little pin, when a voice behind me said :

"Are you going away without drinking your coffee ?"

I turned round and saw my landlord standing close beside me. He was watching my bungling efforts to secure the harness, but he made no movement to assist me.

"I do not want any coffee," I answered.

"No coffee, and no wine ! It would appear that the gentleman is not a great drinker. You have not given your horse much of a rest," he added, presently.

"I am in haste. What have I to pay ?"

"You will take something else," said the landlord ; "a glass of brandy before starting in the wet ?"

"No, nothing more. What have I to pay ?"

"You will at least come in for an instant, and warm your feet at the stove."

"No. Tell me at once how much I am to pay."

Baffled in all his efforts to get me again into the house, my detested landlord had nothing for it but to answer my demand.

"Four litres of oats," he muttered, "a half-truss of hay, breakfast, wine, coffee"—he emphasised the last two words with a malignant grin—"seven francs fifty centimes."

My mare was by this time somehow or other buckled into the shafts, and now I had to get out my purse to pay this demand. My hands were cold, my head was giddy, my sight was dim, and, as I brought out my purse (which was a porte-monnaie, opening with a hinge), I managed while paying the bill to turn the purse over and to drop some gold pieces.

"Gold!" cried the boy who had been helping me to harness the horse: speaking as if by an irresistible impulse.

The landlord made a sudden dart at it, but instantly checked himself.

"People want plenty of gold," he said, "when they make a journey of pleasure."

I felt myself getting worse. I could not pick up the gold pieces as they lay on the ground. I fell on my knees, and my head bowed forward. I could not hit the place where a coin lay; I could see it but I could not guide my fingers to it. Still I did not yield. I got some of the money up, and the stable-boy, who was very officious in assisting me, gave me one or two pieces—to this day, I don't know how many he kept. I cast a hasty glance around, and, seeing no more gold on the ground, raised myself by a desperate effort and scrambled to my place in the carriage. I shook the reins instinctively, and the mare began to move.

The well-trained beast was beginning to trot away as cleverly as usual, when a thought suddenly flashed into my brain, as will sometimes happen when we are just going to sleep—a thought which woke me up like a pistol-shot, and caused me to spring forward and gather up the reins so violently as almost to bring the mare back upon her haunches.

"My dog, my dear little Nelly!" I had left her behind!

To abandon my little favourite was a thing that never entered my head. "No, I must return. I must go back to the horrible place I have just escaped from. He has seen my gold, too, now," I said to myself, as I turned my horse's head with many clumsy efforts; "the men who were drinking in the auberge are gone; and, what is worse than all, I feel more under the influence of the drugs I have swallowed."

As I approached the auberge once more, I remember noticing that its walls looked blacker than ever, that the rain was falling more heavily, that the landlord and the stable-boy were on the steps of the inn, evidently on the look-out for me. One thing more I noticed;—on the road a small speck, as of some vehicle nearing the place.

"I have come back for my dog," said I.

"I know nothing of your dog."

"It is false! I left her shut up in the inner room."

"Go there and find her, then," retorted the man, throwing off all disguise.

"I will," was my answer.

I knew it was a trap to get me into the house; I knew I was lost if I entered it; but I did not care. I descended from the carriage, I clambered up the steps with the aid of the banisters, I heard the barking of my little Nelly as I passed through the outer room and approached the glass-doors, steadying myself as I went by the articles of furniture in the room. I burst the doors open, and my favourite bounded into my arms.

And now I felt that it was too late. As I approached the door that opened to the road, I saw my carriage being led round to the back of the house, and the form of the landlord appeared in the doorway blocking up the passage. I made an effort to push past him, but it was useless. My little Nelly fell out of my arms on the steps outside; the landlord slammed the door heavily; and I fell, without sense or knowledge, at his feet.

* * * * *

It was dark, Gentlemen,—dark and very cold. The little patch of sky I was looking up at, had in it a marvellous number of stars, which would have looked bright but for a blazing planet which seemed to eclipse, in the absence of the moon, all the other luminaries round about it. To lie thus, was in spite of the cold, quite a luxurious sensation. As I turned my head to ease it a little (for it seemed to have been in this position some time), I felt stiff and weak. At this moment, too, I feel a stirring close beside me, and first a cold nose touching my hand, and then a hot tongue licking it. As to my other sensations, I was aware of a gentle rumbling sound, and I could feel that I was being carried slowly along, and that every now and then there was a slight jolt: one of which, perhaps, more marked than the rest, might be the cause of my being awake at all.

Presently, other matters began to dawn upon my mind through the medium of my senses. I could see the regular movement of a horse's ears walking in front of me; surely I saw, too, part of the figure of a man—a pair of sturdy shoulders, the hood of a coat, and a head with a wide-awake hat upon it. I could hear the occasional sounds of encouragement which seemed to emanate from this figure, and which were addressed to the horse. I could hear the tinkling of bells upon the animal's neck. Surely, too, I heard a rumbling sound behind us, and the tread of a horse's feet—just as if there were another vehicle following close upon us. Was there anything more? Yes, in the distance I was able to detect the twinkling of a light or two, as if a town were not far off.

Now, Gentlemen, as I lay and observed all these things, there was such a languor shed over my spirits, such a sense of utter but not unpleasant weakness, that I hardly cared to ask myself what it all meant, or to inquire where I was, or how I came there. A conviction that all was well with me, lay like an anodyne upon my heart, and it was only slowly and gradually that any curiosity as to how I came to be so, developed itself in my brain. I dare say we had been jogging along for a quarter of an hour during which I had been perfectly conscious, before I struggled up into a sitting posture, and recognised the hooded back of the man at the horse's head.

"Dufay?"

The man with the hooded coat who was walking by the side of the horse, suddenly cried out "Wo!" in a sturdy voice; then ran to the back of the carriage and cried out "Wo!" again; and then we came to a stand-still. In another moment he had mounted on the step of the carriage and had taken me cordially by the hand.

"What," he said, "awake at last? Thank Heaven! I had almost begun to despair of you."

"My dear friend, what does all this mean? Where am I? Where did you come from? This is not my calèche, that is not my horse."

"Both are safe behind," said Dufay, heartily; "and having told you so much, I will not utter another word till you are safe and warm at the Lion d'Or. See! There are the lights of the town. Now, not another word." And pulling the horsecloth under which I was lying, more closely over me, my friend dismounted from the step; started the vehicle with the customary cry of "Allons donc!" and a crack of the whip; and we were soon once more in motion.

Castaing Dufay was a man into whose company circumstances had thrown me very often, and with whom I had become intimate from choice. Of the numerous class to which he belonged, those men whose sturdy vehicles and sturdier horses are to be seen standing in the yards and stables of all the inns in provincial France—the class of the commis-voyageurs, or French commercial travellers—Castaing Dufay was more than a favourable specimen. I was very fond of him. In the course of our intimacy, I had been fortunate enough to have the opportunity of being useful to him in matters of some importance. I think, Gentlemen, we like those we have served, quite as well as they like us.

The town lights were, indeed, close by, and it was not long before we turned into the yard of the Lion d'Or and found ourselves in the midst of warmth and brightness, and surrounded by faces which, after the dangers I had passed through, looked perfectly angelic.

I had no idea, till I attempted to move, how weak and dazed I was. I was too far gone for dinner. A bed and a fire were the only things I coveted, and I was soon in possession of both.

I was no sooner snugly ensconced with my head on the pillow, watching the crackling logs as they sparkled—my little Nelly lying outside the counterpane—than my friend seated himself beside me and volunteered to relieve my curiosity as to the circumstances of my escape from the Tête Noire. It was now my turn to refuse to listen; as it had been his before, to refuse to speak.

"Not one word," I said, "till you have had a good dinner, after which you will come up and sit beside me, and tell me all I am longing to know. And stay—you will do one thing more for me, I know; when you come up you will bring a plateful of bones for Nelly; she will not leave me to-night, I swear, to save herself from starving."

"She deserves some dinner," said Dufay, as he left the room, "for I think it is through her instrumentality that you are alive at this moment."

The bliss in which I lay after Dufay had left the room, is known only to those who have passed through some great danger, or who, at least, are newly relieved from some condition of severe and protracted suffering. It was a state of perfect repose and happiness.

When my friend came back, he brought: not only a plate of fowl-bones for Nelly, but a basin of soup for me. When I had finished lapping it up, and while Nelly was still crunching the bones, Dufay spoke as follows:

"I said just now that it was to your little dog you owe the preservation of your life, and I must now tell you how it was. You remember that you left Doulaise this morning——"

"It seems a week ago," I interrupted.

—"This morning," continued Dufay. "Well! You were hardly out of the inn-yard before I drove into it, having made a small stage before breakfast. I heard where you were gone, and, as I was going that way too, I determined to give my horse a rest of a couple of hours, while I breakfasted and transacted some business in the town, and then to set off after you. 'Have you any idea,' I said, as I left the inn at Doulaise, 'whether monsieur meant to stop en route, and if so, where?' The garçon did not know. 'Let me see,' I said, 'the Tête Noire at Mauconseil would be a likely place, wouldn't it?' 'No,' said the boy; 'the house does not enjoy a good character, and no one from here ever stops there.' 'Well,' said I, thinking no more of what he said, 'I shall be sure to find him. I will inquire after him as I go along.'

"The afternoon was getting on, when I came within sight of the inn of the Tête Noire. As you know, I am a little near-sighted, but I saw, as I drew near the auberge, that a conveyance of some kind was being taken round to the yard at the back of the house. This circumstance, however, I should have paid no attention to, had not my attention been suddenly caught by the violent barking of a dog, which seemed to be trying to gain admittance at the closed door of the inn. At a second glance I knew the dog to be yours. Pulling up my horse, I got down and ascended the steps of the auberge. One sniff at my shins was enough to convince Nelly that a friend was at hand, and her excitement as I approached the door was frantic.

"On my entering the house I did not at first see you, but on looking in the direction towards which your dog had hastened as soon as the door was opened, I saw a dark wooden staircase, which led out of one corner of the apartment I was standing in. I saw also, that you, my friend, were being dragged up the stairs in the arms of a very ill-looking man, assisted by (if possible) a still more ill-looking little girl, who had charge of your legs. At sight of me, the man deposited you upon the stairs, and advanced to meet me.

" ' What are you doing with that gentleman ?' I asked.

" ' He is unwell,' replied the ill-looking man, ' and I am helping him up-stairs to bed.'

" ' That gentleman is a friend of mine. What is the meaning of his being in this state ?'

" ' How should I know ?' was the answer; 'I am not the guardian of the gentleman's health.'

" ' Well, then, I am,' said I, approaching the place where you were lying ; ' and I prescribe, to begin with, that he shall leave this place at once.'

" I must own," continued Dufay, "that you were looking horribly ill, and, as I bent over, and felt your hardly fluttering pulse, I felt for a moment doubtful whether it was safe to move you. However, I determined to risk it.

" ' Will you help me,' I said, ' to move this gentleman to his carriage ?'

" ' No,' replied the ruffian, ' he is not fit to travel. Besides, what right have you over him ?'

" ' The right of being his friend.'

" ' How do I know that ?'

" ' Because I tell you so. See, his dog knows me.'

" ' And suppose I decline to accept that as evidence, and refuse to let this gentleman leave my house in his present state of health ?'

" ' You dare not do it.'

" ' Why ?'

" ' Because,' I answered, slowly, ' I should go to the Gendarmerie in the village, and mention under what suspicious circumstances I found my friend here, and because your house has not the best of characters.'

" The man was silent for a moment, as if a little baffled. He seemed, however, determined to try once more.

" ' And suppose I close my doors, and decline to let either of you go ; what is to prevent me ?'

" ' In the first place,' I answered, ' I will effectually prevent your detaining me single-handed. If you have assistance near, I am expected to-night at Francy, and if I do not arrive there, I shall soon be sought out. It was known that I left Doulaise this morning, and most people are aware that there is an auberge on the road which does not bear the best of reputations, and that its name is La Tête Noire. Now, will you help me ?'

" ' No,' replied the savage. ' I will have nothing to do with the affair.'

" It was not an easy task to drag you without assistance from the place where you were lying, out into the open air, down the steps, and to put you into my conveyance which was standing outside ; but I managed to do it. The next thing I had to accomplish, was the feat of driving two carriages and two horses singlehanded. I could see only one way of managing this. I led my own horse round to the gate of the stable-yard, where I could keep my eye upon him, while I went in search of your horse and carriage, which I had to get right without assistance. It was done at last. I fastened your horse's head by a halter, to the back of my carriage, and then leading my own beast by the bridle, I managed to start the procession. And so (though only at a foot pace) we turned our backs upon the Tête Noire. And now you know everything."

"I feel, Castaing, as if I should never be able to think of this adventure, or to speak of it again. It wears, somehow or other, such a ghastly aspect, that I sicken at the mere memory of it."

" Not a bit of it," said Dufay, cheerily ; " you will live to tell it as a stirring tale some winter night, take my word for it."

Gentlemen, the prediction is verified. May the teetotum fall next time with more judgment !

" Wa'al, now !" said Captain Jorgan, rising, with his hand upon the sleeve of his fellow-traveller to keep him down ; " I congratulate you, sir, upon that adventer ; unpleasant at the time, but pleasant to look back upon ; as many adventers in many lives are. Mr. Tredgear, you had a feeling for your money on that occasion, and it went hard on being Stolen Money. It was not a sum of five hundred pound, perhaps ?"

" I wish it had been half as much," was the reply.

" Thank you, sir. Might I ask the question of you that has been already put ? About this place of Lanrean, did you ever hear of any circumstances whatever, that might seem to have a bearing—any how—on that question ?"

" Never."

" Thank you again for a straightfor'ard answer," said the captain, apologetically. " You see, we have been referred to Lanrean to make inquiries, and happening in among the inhabitants present, we use the opportunity. In my country, we always do use opportunities."

" And you turn them to good account, I believe, and prosper ?"

" It's a fact, sir," said the captain, "that we get along. Yes, we get along, sir.—But I stop the teetotum."

It was twirled again, and fell to David Polreath ; an iron-grey man ; "as old as the hills," the captain whispered to young Raybrock, "and as hard as nails.—And I admire," added the captain, glancing about, " whether Unchriscu Penrewen is here, and which is he !"

David Polreath stroked down the long irongrey hair that fell massively upon the shoulders of his large-buttoned coat, and spake thus :

THE question was, Did he throw himself over the cliff of set purpose, or did he lose his way in the dusk and fall over accidentally, or was he pushed over by some person or persons unknown ?

His body was found nearly fifty yards below the fall, caught in the low branches of the trees that overhang the water at the foot of the track down the cliff. It was shockingly bruised and disfigured, so much so as to be hardly recognisable; but for his clothing, and the name on his linen, I doubt whether anybody could have identified him except myself. There was, however, no suspicion of foul play; the signs of rough usage might all have been caused by the body having been driven about amongst the stones that encumber the bed of the river a long way below the fall.

When I speak of the fall, I speak of the Ashenfall, by Ashendell village, within an hour's drive of this house. This, Gentlemen, is for the information of strangers.

He had been seen by many persons about the village during the day; I myself had seen him go up the hill past the parsonage towards the church: which I rather wondered at, considering who was buried there, and how, and why. I will even confess that I watched him; and he went—as I expected he would, since he had the heart to go near the place at all—round to the back of the church where Honor Livingston's grave is; and there he stayed, sitting by himself on the low wall for an hour or more. Sometimes, he turned to look across the valley —many a time and oft I had seen him there before, with Honor beside him, watching, while he sketched the beautiful landscape—and sometimes he had his back to it, and his head down, as if he were watching her grave. Not that there is anything pleasant or comforting to read there, as on the graves of good Christian people who have died in their beds; for, being a suicide, when they buried her on the north side of the church it was at dusk, and without any service, and, of course, no stone was allowed to be put up over it. Our clergyman has talked of having the mound levelled and turfed over, and I wish he would; it always hurts me when I go up to Sunday service, to see that ragged grave lying in the shadow of the wall, for I remember the pretty little lass ever since she could run alone; and though she was passionate, her heart was as good as gold. She had been religiously brought up, and I am quite sure in my own mind, let the coroner's inquest have said what it would, that she was out of herself, and Bedlam-mad when she did it.

The verdict on him was "accidental death," and he had a regular funeral—priest, bell, clerk, and sexton, complete; and there he lies, only a stone's throw from Honor, with a ton or two of granite over him, and an inscription, setting forth what a great man he was in his day, and what mighty engineering works he did at home and abroad, and how he sleeps now in the hope of a joyful resurrection with the just made perfect. These present strangers can read it for themselves; many strangers go up to look at it. His grave is as famous as the Ashenfall itself, and I have known folks come away with tears in their eyes after reading the flourishing inscription: believing it all like gospel, and saying how sad that so distinguished a man should have been cut off in the prime of his

days. But I don't believe it. He was never any more than plain James Lawrence to me— a young fellow who, as a lad, had paddled barelegged over the stones of the river as a guide across for visitors; who had been taken a fancy to by one of them, and decently educated; who had made the most of his luck, and done a clever thing or two in engineering; who had come back amongst us in all his glory, to dazzle most people's eyes, and break little Honor Livingston's heart. The one good thing I know of him was, that he pensioned his poor old mother; but he did not often come near her, and never after Honor Livingston was dead— no, not even in her last illness. It was a marvel to everybody what brought him over here, when we saw him the day before he was found dead; but it was his fate, and he couldn't keep away. That is my view of it. About his death, and the manner of it, all Lanrean had its speculation, and said its say; but I held my peace. I had my opinion, however, and I keep it. I have never seen reason to change it; but, on the contrary, I can show you evidence to establish it. I do not believe he either threw himself over the cliff, or fell over, or was pushed over; no, I believe he was drawn over—drawn over by something below. When you have heard the notes he made in a little book that was found amongst his things after he was dead, you will know what I mean. His cousin gave that book to me, knowing I am curious after odd stories of the neighbourhood; and what I am going to read, is written in his hand. I know his hand well, and certify to it.

PASSAGES FROM JAMES LAWRENCE'S JOURNAL.

London, August 11, 1829.

Honor Livingston has kept her word with me. I saw her last night as plainly as I now see this pen I am writing with, and the inkbottle I have just dipped it into. I saw her standing betwixt the two lights, looking at me, exactly as she looked the last time I saw her alive. I was neither asleep, nor dreaming-awake. I had only drunk a couple of glasses of wine at dinner, and was as much my own man as ever I was in my life. It is all nonsense to talk about fancy and optical delusions, in this case; I saw her with my eyes as distinctly as I ever saw her alive in the body. The hall clock had just struck eight, and it was growing dusk: exactly the time of evening, as I well remember, when she came creeping round by the cottage wall, and saw me through the open window, gathering up my books and making ready to go away from Ashendell. She was the last thought to have come into my mind at that moment, for I was just on the point of lighting my cigar and going out for a stroll, before turning in at the Daltons to chat with Anne. All at once, there she was, Honor herself! I could have sworn it, had I not seen them put her underground just a twelvemonth ago. I could not take my eyes off her; and there she stood, as nearly as I can tell, a minute—but it may have been an hour—and then the place she had filled was empty. I was so much bewildered, and out of myself as it were, that for a while I could neither think of anything, nor hear anything, but the mad heavy throbbing of my own pulses. I cannot say that I was scared exactly; for the time I was completely rapt away; the first actual sensation I had was of my own heart thumping in my breast like a sledge-hammer.

But I can call her up now and analyse her—a wan, vague, misty outline, with Honor's own eyes full upon me. I can almost fancy I hear her asking again, "Is it true you're going, James? You're not really going, James?"

Now, I am not the man to be frightened by a shadow, though that shadow be Honor Livingston, whom they say I as good as murdered. I always had a turn for investigating riddles, spiritual, physiological, and otherwise; and I shall follow this mystery up, and note whether she comes back to me year by year, as she promised. I have never kept a diary of personal matters before, not being one who cares to see spectres of himself, at remote periods of his life, talking to him again of his adventures and misadventures out of yellow old pages that had better never have been written; but this is a marked event worth commemorating, and a well-authenticated ghost-story to me who never believed in ghosts before.

It was a rather spiteful threat of Honor—"I'll haunt you till you come to the Ashenfall, where I'm going now!" I might have stopped her, but it never entered my mind what she meant, until it was done. I did not expect she would make a tragedy of a little love story; she did not look like that sort of thing. She was no ghost, bless her! in the flesh, but as round, rosy, dimpled a little creature as one would wish to see; and what could possess her to throw herself over the fall, Heaven only knows.— Bah! Yes, I know; I need tell no lies here, I need not do any false swearing to myself— the poor little creature loved me, and I wanted her to love me, and I petted and plagued her into loving me, because I was idle, and I had the opportunity; and then I had nothing better to tell her than that I was only in jest— I could not marry her, for I was engaged to another woman. She would not believe it. That sounded, to her, more like jest than the other. And she did not believe it until she saw me making ready to go; and then, all in a moment, I suppose, madness seized her, and she neither knew where she went, nor what she did.

I fancy I can see her now, coming tripping down the fields leading her little brother by the hand, and I fancy I can see the saucy laugh she gave me over her shoulder as I asked her if she had any ripe cherries to sell. She looked the very mischief with those pretty eyes, and I was taken rather aback when she said, "I know you, Jemmy Lawrence." That was the beginning of it. Little Honor and her mother lived next door to mine, and she had not forgotten me though I had been full seven years away. I did not

know her, the gipsy, but I must needs go in and see her that evening; and so we went on until I asked her if she remembered when we went to dame-school together and when she promised to be my little wife? If she remembered! Of course she did, every word of it, and more; and she was so pretty, and the lanes in the summer were so pleasant, that sometimes my fancy did play Anne Dalton false, and I believed I should like Honor better; and I said more than I meant, and she took it all in the grand serious manner.

I was not much to blame. I would not have injured her for the world; she was as good a little soul as ever lived. Love and jealousy, as passions, seem to find their strongholds under thatch. If Phillis, the milkmaid, is disappointed, she drowns herself in the mill-pool; if Lady Clara gets a cross of the heart, she indites a lachrymose sonnet, and marries a gouty peer. If Colin's sweetheart smiles on Lubin, Colin loads his gun and shoots them both; if Sir Harry's fair flouts him, he whistles her down the wind, and goes a-wooing elsewhere. Had little Honor been a fine lady, she would be living still. Oh, the pretty demure lips, and the shy glances and rosy blushes! When I saw Anne Dalton to-day I could not help comparing her frigid gentility with poor Honor. Anne loves herself better than she will ever love any man alive. But then I know she is the kind of wife to help a man up in the world, and that is the kind of wife for me.

Honor Livingston lying on her little bed, and her blind mother feeling her cold dead face! I wish I had never seen it. I would have given the world to keep away, but something compelled me to go in and look at her; and I did feel then, as if I had killed her. Last night she was a shadowy essence of this drowned Ophelia and of her living self. She was like, yet unlike; but I knew it was Honor; and I suppose, if she has her will, wherever her restless spirit may be condemned to bide between whiles—on the tenth of August she will always come back to me, and haunt me until I go to her.

Hastings, August 11, 1830.

Again! I had forgotten the day—forgotten everything about that wretched business of poor Honor Livingston, when last night I saw her.

Anne and I were sitting together out in the verandah, talking of all sorts of common-place things—our neighbours' affairs, money, this, that, and the other—the sea was looking beautiful, and I was on the point of proposing a row by moonlight, when Anne said, "How lovely the evenings are, James, in this place. Look at the sky over the down, how clear it is!" Turning my head, I saw Honor standing on the grass only a few paces off, her shadowy shape quite distinct against the reds and purples of the clouds.

Anne clutched my hand with a sudden cry, for she was looking at my face all the time, and asked me, passionately, what I saw. With that, Honor was gone, and, passing my hand over my eyes, I put my wife off with an excuse about a spasm at my heart. And, indeed, it was no lie to say so, for this visitation gave me a terrible shock.

Anne insisted on my seeing the doctor. "It must be something dreadful, if not dangerous, that could make you look in that way; you had an awful face, James, for a moment."

I begged her not to talk about it, assured her that it was a thing of very rare recurrence with me, and that there was no cure for it. But this did not pacify her, and this morning no peace could be had until Dr. Hutchinson was sent for and she had given the old gentleman her own account of me. He said he would talk to me by-and-by. And when he got me by myself, I cannot tell how it was, but he absolutely contrived to worm the facts out of me, and I was fool enough to let him do it. He looked at me very oddly, with a sort of suspicious scrutiny in his eye; but I understood him, and said, laughing, " No, doctor; no, there is nothing wrong here," tapping my forehead as I spoke.

"I should say not, except this fancy for seeing ghosts," replied he, dryly. But I perceived, all the time he was with me, that I was the object of a furtive and carefully dissembled observation, which was excessively trying. I could with difficulty keep my temper under it, and I believe he saw the struggle.

I fancy he wanted to have some talk with Anne by herself; but I prevented that, by never losing sight of him until he was safely off the premises. If he proposed a private interview while I was out alone, I prevented that, too, by immediately ordering Anne to pack up our traps, and coming back to town that very day. I have not been well since. I feel out of spirits, bored, worried, sick of everything. If the feeling does not leave me, in spite of all Anne may say, I shall take that offer to go to South America, and start by the next packet. I should like to see Dr. Hutchinson's face when he calls at our lodgings to visit his patient, and finds the bird flown.

London, August 20, 1830.

This wretched state of things does not cease. One day I feel in full, firm, clear possession of my soul; and the next, perhaps, I am hurried to and fro with the most tormenting fancies. I see shadows of Honor wherever I turn, and she is no longer motionless as before, but beckons me with her hand, until I tremble in every limb. My heart is sick almost to death. For three days now, I have had no rest. I cannot sleep at nights for hideous dreams; and Anne watches me stealthily, I see, and never remains alone with me longer than she can help. I can perceive that she is afraid of me, and that she suspects something, without exactly knowing what. To-day she must needs suggest my seeing a doctor here, and when I replied that I was going to South America, she told me I was not fit for it, in such a contemptuous tone of provocation that I lifted my hand and struck her. Then she quailed, and while shrinking under my eyes, she said, " James, your conduct

is that of a madman!" Since then, I know she sits with me in silent terror, longing to escape and find some one to listen to her grievances. But I shall keep strict ward that she does nothing of the kind. I will not have my foes of my own household, and no spying relatives shall come between us to put asunder those whom God has joined together.

Acapulco, March 17, 1831.

It is six months since I wrote the above. In the interval I have been miserably ill, grievously tormented both in mind and body; but now that I have got safely away from them all, with the Atlantic between myself and my wicked wife, whose conduct towards me I will never forgive, I can collect my powers of mind, and bend them again to my work. Burton came out in the same ship with me to engage in the same enterprise. After a few days' rest we intend setting out on our journey to the mining districts, where we are to act. My head feels perfectly light and clear, all my impressions are distinct and vivid again, and I can get through a hard day's close study without inconvenience. There was nothing but my miserable liver to blame, and when that was set right, all my imaginary phantoms disappeared. Umpleby said it had been coming on gradually for months, and that there was nothing at all extraordinary in my delusions; my diseased state was one always so attended more or less. And Anne, in her cowardly malignity, would have consigned me for life to a lunatic asylum! It was Umpleby who saved me, and I have put his name down in my will for a handsome remembrance. As for Anne, she has chosen to return to her family, and they may keep her; she will never see my face again, of my free will, as long as I live.

The picturesqueness of this place is not noteworthy in any high degree. The harbour is enclosed by a chain of mountains, and has two entrances formed by the island of Roquetta; the castle of St. Diego commands the town and the bay, standing on a spur of the hills. Burton has been to and fro on his rambles ever since we landed; but I find the heat too great for much exertion, and when we begin our journey into the interior I shall have need of all my forces; therefore, better husband them now.

Mexico, April 24, 1831.

We are better off here than we anticipated. Burton has found an old fellow-pupil engaged as engineering tutor in the School of Mines, and there are civilised amusements which we neither of us had any hope of finding. The city is full of ancient relics, and Burton is on foot exploring, day by day. I prefer the living interests of this strange place, and sometimes early in the morning I betake myself to the market-place, and watch the Indians dress their stalls. No matter what they sell, they decorate their shops with fresh herbs and flowers until they are sheltered under a bower of verdure. They display their fruit in open basket-work, laying the pears and raisins below, and covering them above with odorous flowers. An artist might make a pretty picture here, when the Indians arrive at sunrise in their boats loaded with the produce of their floating gardens. Next week, Burton, his friend, and I, are to set out for the mines of Moran and Real del Monte. I should have preferred to delay our journey a while longer for reasons of my own, but Burton presses, and feels we have already delayed longer than enough.

Moran, July 4, 1831.

I am sick of this place, but our business here is now on the verge of completion, and in a few days we start on our expedition to the mines of Guanamato. The director, Burton, and myself, are all of opinion that immense advantages are to be gained by improving the working of the mines, which is, at present, in a very defective condition. There is great mortality amongst the Indians, who are the beasts of burden of the mines; they carry on their backs, loads of metal of from two hundred and fifty to three hundred and fifty pounds at a time, ascending and descending thousands of steps, in files which contain old men of seventy, and mere children. I have not been very well here, having had some return of old symptoms, but under proper treatment they dispersed; however, I shall be thankful to be on the move again.

Pascuaro, August 11, 1831.

Can any man evade his thoughts, impalpable curses sitting on his heart, mocking like fiends? I cannot evade mine. All yesterday I was haunted by a terrible anxiety and dread. At every turn, at every moment, I expected to see Honor Livingston appear before me, but I did not see her. The day and the night passed, and I was freed from that great horror—how great I had not realised until its hour had gone and left no trace. This morning I am myself again; my spirits revive; I have escaped my enemy, and have proved that it was, indeed, but a subtle emanation of my own diseased body and mind. But these thoughts, these troublesome persistent thoughts, how combat them? Burton, very observant of me at all times, was yesterday watchful as an inquisitor; he said he hoped I was not going to have the frightful fever which is prevailing here, but I know he meant something else. I have not a doubt now, that Anne and all that confederacy warned him before we set sail, to beware of me, for I had been mad; that is the cursed lie they set abroad. Mad! All the world's mad, or on the way to it!

But if Honor had come back to me yesterday, we might have gone and have looked down together into hell, through the ovens of Jorulla. The missionaries cursed this frightful place, generations since; and it is accursed, if ever land was. Nothing more awful than this desolate burning waste, which the seas could not quench. When I remember it, and all I underwent yesterday, the confusion and horror return upon me again, and my brain swerves like the brain of a drunken man. I will write no more

—sufficient to record that the appointed time came and went, and Honor Livingston did not keep her word with me.

New Orleans, February, 1832.

I left Burton still in Mexico, and came here alone. His care and considerateness were more than I could put up with, and after two or three ineffectual remonstrances, we came to a violent rupture, and I determined to throw up my engagement, rather than carry it out in conjunction with such a man. There was no avoiding the quarrel. Was I to be tutored day by day, and the wine-bottle removed out of my reach? He dared to tell me that when I was cool, clear —myself, in short—there was no man my master in our profession; but that when I had drunk freely I was unmanageable as a lunatic! A lie, of course; but unscrupulous persecutors are difficult to circumvent. Anne's malice pursues me even here. When I was out yesterday, my footsteps were dogged pertinaciously wherever I went, and perhaps an account of my doings will precede me home; but if they do, I defy them all to do their worst.

Ashendell, August 9, 1839.

This old book turned up to-day, amongst some traps that have lain by in London all the years that I have spent, first in Spain and afterwards in Russia. What fool's-talk it is; but I suppose it was true at the time. I know I was in a wretched condition while I was in Mexico and in the States, but I have been sane enough and sound enough ever since the illness I had at Baltimore. To prove how little hold on me my ancient horrors have retained, I find myself at Ashendell in the very season of the year when Honor Livingston destroyed herself—to-morrow is the anniversary of her death. So I take my enemy by the throat, and crush him! These fantastical maladies will not stand against a determined will. At Moscow, at Cherson, at Archangel, the tenth of August has come and gone, unmarked. Honor failed of her threat everywhere except at Lisbon. I saw her there twice, just before we sailed. I saw her, when we were off that coast where we so nearly escaped wreck, rising and falling upon the waves. I saw her in London, that day I appointed to see Anne. But I know what it means: it means that I must put myself in Umpleby's hands for a few weeks, and that the shadows will forthwith vanish. Shadows they are, out of my own brain, and they take the shape of Honor because I have let her become a fixed idea in my mind. Yet it is very strange that the last time she appeared to me, I heard her speak. I fancied she said that it was Almost time; and then louder, "I'll haunt you, James, until you come to the Ashenfall, where I am going now!" And with that she vanished. Fancy plays strange tricks with us, and makes cowards of us almost as cleverly as conscience.

August 10.

I have had a very unpleasant impression on me all day. I wish I had resisted Linchley's persuasions more steadily. I ought never to have come down here again. The excitement of its miserable recollections is too much for me. The man at the inn called me by my name this morning, and said he recollected me—looking up towards the church as he spoke. Damn him! All day I seem to have been acting against my will. What should possess me to go there, this afternoon? Round about among the graves, until I came to the grassy hillock on the north side of the church, where they buried Honor that night, without a prayer. I sat down en the low wall, and looked across to the hills beyond the river, listening to the monotonous sing-song of the fall. I would give all I possess to-day, to be able to tread back or to untread a score of the years of my life. It seems such a blank; of all I planned and schemed, how little have I accomplished! Watching by Honor's grave, I fell to thinking of her. What had either of us done that we should be so wretched? Is it part and parcel of the great injustice of life, that some must suffer so signally while others escape? The coarse grass is never cut at the north side of the church, nettles and brambles grow about the grave. Honor was mad, poor soul; they might have given her a prayer for rest, if they were forbidden to believe she died in hope. I prayed for her to-day—more need, perhaps, to pray for myself—and then there came a crazed whirl in my brain, and I set off to find Linchley. As I came down near the water, the fall sounded very tumultuous; it was sultry hot, and I should have liked to turn down by the river, but I said, "No, it is the tenth of August! If I am to meet Honor Livingston to-day, I'll not meet her by Ashenfall!" So I came home to our lodgings, to find that Linchley had gone over to Warfe, and had left a message that he should not return until to-morrow. I have the night before me alone; it is not like an English night at all; it is like the nights I remember at Cadiz, which always heralded a tremendous storm. And I think we shall have a storm here, too, before the morning.

Those were the last words James Lawrence ever wrote, Gentlemen. Further than this, no man can speak of his death; it is plain to me that one of his mad fits was coming on before he left Lisbon; that it grew and increased until he came here; and that here it reached its climax and urged him to his death. I believe in the ghosts James Lawrence saw, as I believe in the haunting power of any great misdeed that has driven a fellow-creature into deadly sin.

When David Polreath had finished, the chairman gave the teetotum such a swift and sudden twirl, to be beforehand with any interruption, that it twirled among all the glasses and into all corners of the table, and finally, flew off the table and lodged in Captain Jorgan's waistcoat.

"A kind of a judgment!" said the captain, taking it out. "What's to be done now? I know no story, except Down Easters, and they didn't happen to myself, or any one of my acquaintance, and you couldn't enjoy 'em without going out of your minds first. And perhaps the company ain't prepared to do that?"

The chairman interposed by rising and declaring it to be his perroud perrivilege to stop preliminary observations.

"Wa'al," said the captain, "I defer to the President—which an't at all what they do in my country, where they lay into him, head, limbs, and body." Here he slapped his leg. "But I beg to ask a preliminary question. Colonel Polreath has read from a diary. Might I read from a pipe-light?"

The chairman requested explanation.

"The history of the pipe-light," said the captain, "is just this:—that it's verses, and was made on the voyage home by a passenger I brought over. And he was a quiet crittur of a middle-aged man with a pleasant countenance. And he wrote it on the head of a cask. And he was a most eternal time about it tew. And he blotted it as if he had wrote it in a continual squall of ink. And then he took an indigestion, and I physicked him for want of a better doctor. And then to show his liking for me he copied it out fair, and gave it to me for a pipe-light. And it ain't been lighted yet, and that's a fact."

"Let it be read," said the chairman.

"With thanks to Colonel Polreath for setting the example," pursued the captain, "and with apologies to the Honourable A. Parvis and the whole of the present company for this passenger's having expressed his mind in verses—which he may have done along of bein' sea-sick, and he was very—the pipe-light, unrolled, comes to this:

We sit by the fire so wide and red,
   With the dance of the young within,
Who have yet small learning of cold and dread,
   And of sorrow no more than of sin;
Nor dream of a night on a sleepless bed
Of waves, with their terrible wrecks o'erspread.

We sit round the hearth as red as gold,
   And the legends beloved we tell,
How battles were won by the nobles bold,
   Where hamlets of villains fell:
And we praise our God, while we cut the bread,
And share the wine round, for our heroes dead.

And we talk of the Kings, those strong proud men,
   Who ravaged, confessed, and died;
And of churls who rabbled them oft and again,
   Perchance with a kindred pride—
Though the Kings built churches to pierce the sky,
And the rabbling churls in the cross-road lie.

Yet 'twixt the despot and slave half-free,
   Old Truth may have message clear;
Since the hard black yew, and the lithe young tree,
Belong to an age—and a year,
And though distant in might and in leaf they be,
   In right of the woods, they are near.

And old Truth's message, perchance, may be:
"Believe in thy kind, whate'er the degree,
Be it King on his throne, or serf on his knee,
While Our Lord showers light, in his bounty free,
On the rock and the vale—on the sand and the sea."

They are singing within, with their voices dear,
  To the tunes which are dear as well ;
And we sit and dream while the words we hear,
  Having tale of our own to tell—
Of a far midnight on the terrible sea,
Which comes back on the tune of their blithe old glee.

As old as the hills, and as old as the sky,—
  As the King on his throne,—as the serf on his
    knee,
  A song wherein rich can with poor agree,
With its chorus to make them laugh or cry—
Which the young are singing, with no thought nigh,
  Of a night on a terrible sea :
    " I care for nobody ; no, not I,
      Since nobody cares for me."

The storm had its will. There was wreck—there was
    flight
O'er an ocean of Alps, through the pitch-black
    night,
When a good ship sank, and a few got free,
To cope in their boat with the terrible sea.

And when the day broke, there was blood on the sea,
  From the wild hot eye of the sun outshed,
For the heaven was a-flame as with fire from Hell,
  And a scorching calm on the waters fell,
As if Ruin had won, and with fiendish glee,
  Sailed forth in his galley to number the dead.

And they rowed their boat o'er the terrible sea,
As mute as a crew made of ghosts might be :
For the best in his heart had not manhood to say,
That the land was five hundred miles away.

A day—and a week—There was bread for one man;
  The water was dry. And on this, the few
Who were rowing their boat o'er the terrible sea,
To murmur, to curse, and to crave began.
  And how 'twas agreed on, no one knew,
But the feeble and famished and scorched by the
    sun,
With his pitiless eye, drew lots to agree,
What their hideous morrow of meat must be.

O then were the faces frightful to read,
  Of ravening hope. and of cowardly pride
That lies to the last, its sharp terror to hide ;
  And a stillness as though 'twere some game of the
    Dead,
    While they waited the number their lot to decide—
There were nine in that boat on the terrible sea,
And he who drew NINE, was the victim to be.

You may think what a ghastly shiver there ran,
From mate to his mate, as the doom began.

SIX—had a wife with a wild rose cheek ;
  Two—a brave boy, not a year yet old ;
EIGHT—his last sister, lame and weak,
  Who quivered with palsy more than with cold.

You may think what a breath the respited drew,
And how wildly still, sat the rest of the crew ;
How the voice as it called spoke hoarser and slower ;
The number it next dared to speak was—FOUR.

'Twas the rude black man, who had handled an oar
  The best on that terrible sea of the few.
And ugly and grim in the sunshine glare
  Were his thick parched lips, and his dull small
    eyes,
And the tangled fleece of his rusty hair—
  'Ere the next of the breathless death-lot drew,
  His shout like a sword pierced the silence through.

" Let the play end, with your Number Four.
  What need to draw ? Live along, you few
Who have hopes to save and have wives to cry
  O'er the cradles of children free !
What matter if folk without home should die,
  And be eaten by land or sea ?
    I care for nobody ; no, not I,
      Since nobody cares for me !"

And with that, a knife—and a heart struck through—
  And the warm red blood, and the cold black clay,
And the famine withdrawn from among the few,
  By their horrible meal for another day !

So the eight, thus fed, came at last to land,
  And the tale of their shipmate told,
As of water found in the burning sand,
  Which braves not the thirsty, cold.
But the love of the listener, safe and free,
Goes forth to that slave on that terrible sea.

For, fancies from hearth and from home will stray,
  Though within are the dance and the song ;
And a grave tale told, if the tune be gay,
  Says little to scare the young.
While they sing, with their voices clear as can be,
Having called, once more, for the blithe old glee—
    " I care for nobody, no, not I, ,
      Since nobody cares for me."

But the careless tune, it saith to the old,
Who sit by the hearth as red as gold,
When they think of their tale of the terrible sea :
" *Believe in thy kind, whate'er the degree,*
Be it King on his throne, or serf on his knee,
While Our Lord showers good from his bounty free,
Over storm, over calm, over land, over sea."

Mr. Parvis had so greatly disquieted the
minds of the Gentlemen King Arthurs for some
minutes, by snoring with strong symptoms of
apoplexy—which, in a mild form, was his normal
state of health—that it was now deemed expe-
dient to wake him and entreat him to allow himself to be escorted home. Mr. Parvis's reply to
this friendly suggestion could not be placed on
record without the aid of several dashes, and is
therefore omitted. It was conceived in a spirit
of the profoundest irritation, and executed with
vehemence, contempt, scorn, and disgust. There
was nothing for it, but to let the excellent
gentleman alone, and he fell without loss of time
into a defiant slumber.

The teetotum being twirled again, so buzzed
and bowed in the direction of the young fisherman, that Captain Jorgan advised him to be
bright and prepare for the worst. But, it started
off at a tangent, late in its career, and fell before
a well-looking bearded man (one who made
working drawings for machinery, the captain was
informed by his next neighbour), who promptly
took it up like a challenger's glove.

" Oswald Penrewen !" said the chairman.

" Here's Unchris'en at last !" the captain
whispered Alfred Raybrock. " Unchris'en goes
ahead, right smart ; don't he ?"

He did, without one introductory word.

MINE is my brother's Ghost Story. It happened to my brother about thirty years ago,

while he was wandering, sketch-book in hand, among the High Alps, picking up subjects for an illustrated work on Switzerland. Having entered the Oberland by the Brunig Pass, and filled his portfolio with what he used to call "bits" from the neighbourhood of Meyringen, he went over the Great Scheideck to Grindelwald, where he arrived one dusky September evening, about three-quarters of an hour after sunset. There had been a fair that day, and the place was crowded. In the best inn there was not an inch of space to spare—there were only two inns at Grindelwald, thirty years ago—so my brother went to one at the end of the covered bridge next the church, and there, with some difficulty, obtained the promise of a pile of rugs and a mattress, in a room which was already occupied by three other travellers.

The Adler was a primitive hostelry, half farm, half inn, with great rambling galleries outside, and a huge general room, like a barn. At the upper end of this room stood long stoves, like metal counters, laden with steaming-pans, and glowing underneath like furnaces. At the lower end, smoking, supping, and chatting, were congregated some thirty or forty guests, chiefly mountaineers, char drivers, and guides. Among these my brother took his seat, and was served, like the rest, with a bowl of soup, a platter of beef, a flagon of country wine, and a loaf made of Indian corn. Presently, a huge St. Bernard dog came and laid his nose upon my brother's arm. In the mean time he fell into conversation with two Italian youths, bronzed and dark-eyed, near whom he happened to be seated. They were Florentines. Their names, they told him, were Stefano and Battisto. They had been travelling for some months on commission, selling cameos, mosaics, sulphur casts, and the like pretty Italian trifles, and were now on their way to Interlaken and Geneva. Weary of the cold North, they longed, like children, for the moment which should take them back to their own blue hills and grey-green olives; to their workshop on the Ponte Vecchio, and their home down by the Arno.

It was quite a relief to my brother, on going up to bed, to find that these youths were to be two of his fellow-lodgers. The third was already there, and sound asleep, with his face to the wall. They scarcely looked at this third. They were all tired, and all anxious to rise at daybreak, having agreed to walk together over the Wengern Alp as far as Lauterbrunnen. So, my brother and the two youths exchanged a brief good night, and, before many minutes, were all as far away in the land of dreams as their unknown companion.

My brother slept profoundly—so profoundly that, being roused in the morning by a clamour of merry voices, he sat up dreamily in his rugs, and wondered where he was.

"Good day, signor," cried Battisto. "Here is a fellow-traveller going the same way as ourselves."

"Christien Baumann, native of Kandersteg,

musical-box maker by trade, stands five feet eleven in his shoes, and is at monsieur's service to command," said the sleeper of the night before.

He was as fine a young fellow as one would wish to see. Light, and strong, and well proportioned, with curling brown hair, and bright, honest eyes that seemed to dance at every word he uttered.

"Good morning," said my brother. "You were asleep last night when we came up."

"Asleep! I should think so, after being all day in the fair, and walking from Meyringen the evening before. What a capital fair it was!"

"Capital, indeed," said Battisto. "We sold cameos and mosaics yesterday, for nearly fifty francs."

"Oh, you sell cameos and mosaics, you two! Show me your cameos, and I will show you my musical boxes. I have such pretty ones, with coloured views of Geneva and Chillon on the lids, playing two, four, six, and even eight tunes. Bah! I will give you a concert!"

And with this he unstrapped his pack, displayed his little boxes on the table, and wound them up, one after the other, to the delight of the Italians.

"I helped to make them myself, every one," said he, proudly. "Is it not pretty music? I sometimes set one of them when I go to bed at night, and fall asleep listening to it. I am sure, then, to have pleasant dreams! But let us see your cameos. Perhaps I may buy one for Marie, if they are not too dear. Marie is my sweetheart, and we are to be married next week."

"Next week!" exclaimed Stefano. "That is very soon. Battisto has a sweetheart also, up at Impruneta; but they will have to wait a long time before they can buy the ring."

Battisto blushed like a girl.

"Hush, brother!" said he. "Show the cameos to Christien, and give your tongue a holiday!"

But Christien was not so to be put off.

"What is her name?" said he. "Tush! Battisto, you must tell me her name! Is she pretty? Is she dark, or fair? Do you often see her when you are at home? Is she very fond of you? Is she as fond of you as Marie is of me?"

"Nay, how should I know that?" asked the soberer Battisto. "She loves me, and I love her—that is all."

"And her name?"

"Margherita."

"A charming name! And she is herself as pretty as her name, I'll engage. Did you say she was fair?"

"I said nothing about it one way or the other," said Battisto, unlocking a green box clamped with iron, and taking out tray after tray of his pretty wares. "There! Those pictures all inlaid in little bits are Roman mosaics—these flowers on a black ground are Florentine. The ground is of hard dark stone, and the flowers are made of thin slices of jasper, onyx, cornelian, and so forth. Those forget-me-nots, for instance, are bits of turquoise, and that poppy is cut from a piece of coral."

" I like the Roman ones best," said Christien. " What place is that with all the arches?"

. " This is the Coliseum, and the one next to it is St. Peter's. But we Florentines care little for the Roman work. It is not half so fine or so valuable as ours. The Romans make their mosaics of composition."

" Composition or no, I like the little landscapes best," said Christien. " There is a lovely one, with a pointed building, and a tree, and mountains at the back. How I should like that one for Marie!"

" You may have it for eight francs," replied Battisto; " we sold two of them yesterday for ten each. It represents the tomb of Caius Cestius, near Rome."

" A tomb!" echoed Christien, considerably dismayed. " Diable! That would be a dismal present to one's bride."

" She would never guess that it was a tomb, if you did not tell her," suggested Stefano.

Christien shook his head.

" That would be next door to deceiving her," said he.

" Nay," interposed my brother, "the owner of that tomb has been dead these eighteen or nineteen hundred years. One almost forgets that he was ever buried in it."

" Eighteen or nineteen hundred years? Then he was a heathen?"

" Undoubtedly, if by that you mean that he lived before Christ."

Christien's face lighted up immediately.

" Oh, that settles the question," said he, pulling out his little canvas purse, and paying his money down at once. "A heathen's tomb is as good as no tomb at all. I'll have it made into a brooch for her, at Interlaken. Tell me, Battisto, what shall you take home to Italy for your Margherita?"

Battisto, laughed, and chinked his eight francs.

" That depends on trade," said he; " if we make good profits between this and Christmas, I may take her a Swiss muslin from Berne; but we have already been away seven months, and we have hardly made a hundred francs over and above our expenses."

And with this, the talk turned upon general matters, the Florentines locked away their treasures, Christien restrapped his pack, and my brother and all went down together, and breakfasted in the open air outside the inn.

It was a magnificent morning: cloudless and sunny, with a cool breeze that rustled in the vine upon the porch, and flecked the table with shifting shadows of green leaves. All around and about them stood the great mountains, with their blue-white glaciers bristling down to the verge of the pastures, and the pine-woods creeping darkly up their sides. To the left, the Wetterhorn; to the right, the Eigher; straight before them, dazzling and imperishable, like an

obelisk of frosted silver, the Schreckhorn, or Peak of Terror. Breakfast over, they bade farewell to their hostess, and, mountain-staff in hand, took the path to the Wengern Alp. Half in light, half in shadow, lay the quiet valley, dotted over with farms, and traversed by a torrent that rushed, milk-white, from its prison in the glacier. The three lads walked briskly in advance, their voices chiming together every now and then in chorus of laughter. Somehow my brother felt sad. He lingered behind, and, plucking a little red flower from the bank, watched it hurry away with the torrent, like a life on the stream of time. Why was his heart so heavy, and why were their hearts so light?

As the day went on, my brother's melancholy, and the mirth of the young men, seemed to increase. Full of youth and hope, they talked of the joyous future, and built up pleasant castles in the air. Battisto, grown more communicative, admitted that to marry Margherita, and become a master mosaicist, would fulfil the dearest dream of his life. Stefano, not being in love, preferred to travel. Christien, who seemed to be the most prosperous, declared that it was his darling ambition to rent a farm in his native Kander Valley, and lead the patriarchal life of his fathers. As for the musical-box trade, he said, one should live in Geneva to make it answer; and, for his part, he loved the pine-forests and the snow-peaks, better than all the towns in Europe. Marie, too, had been born among the mountains, and it would break her heart, if she thought she were to live in Geneva all her life, and never see the Kander Thal again. Chatting thus, the morning wore on to noon, and the party rested awhile in the shade of a clump of gigantic firs festooned with trailing banners of grey-green moss.

Here they ate their lunch, to the silvery music of one of Christien's little boxes, and by-and-by heard the sullen echo of an avalanche far away on the shoulder of the Jungfrau.

Then they went on again in the burning afternoon, to heights where the Alp-rose fails from the sterile steep, and the brown lichen grows more and more scantily among the stones. Here, only the bleached and barren skeletons of a forest of dead pines varied the desolate monotony; and high on the summit of the pass, stood a little solitary inn, between them and the sky.

At this inn they rested again, and drank to the health of Christien and his bride, in a jug of country wine. He was in uncontrollable spirits, and shook hands with them all, over and over again.

" By nightfall to-morrow," said he, " I shall hold her once more in my arms! It is now nearly two years since I came home to see her, at the end of my apprenticeship. Now I am foreman, with a salary of thirty francs a week, and well able to marry."

" Thirty francs a week!" echoed Battisto. " Corpo di Bacco! that is a little fortune."

Christien's face beamed.

_ " Yes," said he, "we shall be very happy; and,

by-and-by—who knows?—we may end our days in
the Kander Thal, and bring up our children to
succeed us. Ah! If Marie knew that I should be
there to-morrow night, how delighted she would
be!"

"How so, Christien?" said my brother. "Does
she not expect you?"

"Not a bit of it. She has no idea that I can
be there till the day after to-morrow—nor could
I, if I took the road all round by Unterseen and
Frütigen. I mean to sleep to-night at Lauterbrunnen, and to-morrow morning shall strike
across the Tschlingel glacier to Kandersteg. If I
rise a little before daybreak, I shall be at home
by sunset."

At this moment the path took a sudden turn,
and began to descend in sight of an immense per-
spective of very distant valleys. Christien flung
his cap into the air, and uttered a great shout.

"Look!" said he, stretching out his arms as if
to embrace all the dear familiar scene: "O! Look!
There are the hills and woods of Interlaken, and
here, below the precipices on which we stand, lies
Lauterbrunnen! God be praised, who has made
our native land so beautiful!"

The Italians smiled at each other, thinking their
own Arno valley far more fair; but my brother's
heart warmed to the boy, and echoed his thanks-
giving in that spirit which accepts all beauty as
a birthright and an inheritance. And now their
course lay across an immense plateau, all rich
with corn-fields and meadows, and studded with
substantial homesteads built of old brown wood,
with huge sheltering eaves, and strings of Indian
corn hanging like golden ingots along the carven
balconies. Blue whortleberries grew beside the
footway, and now and then they came upon a wild
gentian, or a star-shaped immortelle. Then the
path became a mere zigzag on the face of the pre-
cipice, and in less than half an hour they reached
the lowest level of the valley. The glowing afternoon had not yet faded from the uppermost pines,
when they were all dining together in the parlour
of a little inn looking to the Jungfrau. In the
evening my brother wrote letters, while the three
lads strolled about the village. At nine o'clock
they bade each other good night, and went to
their several rooms.

Weary as he was, my brother found it impossible to sleep. The same unaccountable melancholy still possessed him, and when at last he
dropped into an uneasy slumber, it was but to
start over and over again from frightful dreams,
faint with a nameless terror. Towards morning,
he fell into a profound sleep, and never woke until
the day was fast advancing towards noon. He
then found, to his regret, that Christien had long
since gone. He had risen before daybreak, breakfasted by candlelight, and started off in the grey
dawn—"as merry," said the host, "as a fiddler
at a fair."

Stefano and Battisto were still waiting to see
my brother, being charged by Christien with a
friendly farewell message to him, and an invita-
tion to the wedding. They, too, were asked, and

meant to go; so, my brother agreed to meet them
at Interlaken on the following Tuesday, whence
they might walk to Kandersteg by easy stages,
reaching their destination on the Thursday morning, in time to go to church with the bridal party.
My brother then bought some of the little Florentine cameos, wished the two boys every good fortune, and watched them down the road till he
could see them no longer.

Left now to himself, he wandered out with
his sketch-book, and spent the day in the
upper valley; at sunset, he dined alone in his
chamber, by the light of a single lamp. This meal
despatched, he drew nearer to the fire, took out
a pocket edition of Goethe's Essays on Art, and
promised himself some hours of pleasant reading.
(Ah, how well I know that very book, in its faded
cover, and how often I have heard him describe
that lonely evening!) The night had by this
time set in cold and wet. The damp logs
spluttered on the hearth, and a wailing wind
swept down the valley, bearing the rain in sudden
gusts against the panes. My brother soon found
that to read was impossible. His attention
wandered incessantly. He read the same sentence
over and over again, unconscious of its meaning,
and fell into long trains of thought leading far
into the dim past.

Thus the hours went by, and at eleven o'clock
he heard the doors closing below, and the household retiring to rest. He determined to yield
no longer to this dreaming apathy. He threw
on fresh logs, trimmed the lamp, and took
several turns about the room. Then he opened
the casement, and suffered the rain to beat against
his face, and the wind to ruffle his hair, as it
ruffled the acacia leaves in the garden below.
Some minutes passed thus, and when, at length,
he closed the window and came back into the room,
his face and hair and all the front of his shirt
were thoroughly saturated. To unstrap his knapsack and take out a dry shirt was, of course, his
first impulse—to drop the garment, listen eagerly,
and start to his feet, breathless and bewildered,
was the next.

For, borne fitfully upon the outer breeze,
now sweeping past the window, now dying in the
distance, he heard a well-remembered strain of
melody, subtle and silvery as the "sweet airs"
of Prospero's isle, and proceeding unmistakably,
from the musical-box which had, the day before,
accompanied the lunch under the fir-trees of the
Wengern Alp!

Had Christien come back, and was it thus that
he announced his return? If so, where was he?
Under the window? Outside in the corridor?
Sheltering in the porch, and waiting for admittance? My brother threw open the casement
again, and called him by his name.

"Christien! Is that you?"

All without was intensely silent. He could
hear the last gust of wind and rain moaning
farther and farther away upon its wild course
down the valley, and the pine trees shivering,
like living things.

"Christien!" he said again, and his own voice seemed to echo strangely on his ear. "Speak! Is it you?"

Still no one answered. He leaned out into the dark night; but could see nothing—not even the outline of the porch below. He began to think that his imagination had deceived him, when suddenly the strain burst forth again;—this time, apparently in his own chamber.

As he turned, expecting to find Christien at his elbow, the sounds broke off abruptly, and a sensation of intensest cold seized him in every limb—not the mere chill of nervous terror, not the mere physical result of exposure to wind and rain, but a deadly freezing of every vein, a paralysis of every nerve, an appalling consciousness that in a few moments more the lungs must cease to play, and the heart to beat! Powerless to speak or stir, he closed his eyes, and believed that he was dying.

This strange faintness lasted but a few seconds. Gradually the vital warmth returned, and, with it, strength to close the window, and stagger to a chair. As he did so, he found the breast of his shirt all stiff and frozen, and the rain clinging in solid icicles upon his hair.

He looked at his watch. It had stopped at twenty minutes before twelve. He took his thermometer from the chimney-piece, and found the mercury at sixty-eight. Heavenly powers! How were these things possible in a temperature of sixty-eight degrees, and with a large fire blazing on the hearth?

He poured out half a tumbler of cognac, and drank it at a draught. Going to bed was out of the question. He felt that he dared not sleep—that he scarcely dared to think. All he could do, was, to change his linen, pile on more logs, wrap himself in his blankets, and sit all night in an easy-chair before the fire.

My brother had not long sat thus, however, before the warmth, and probably the nervous reaction, drew him off to sleep. In the morning he found himself lying on the bed, without being able to remember in the least how or when he reached it.

It was again a glorious day. The rain and wind were gone, and the Silverhorn at the end of the valley lifted its head into an unclouded sky. Looking out upon the sunshine, he almost doubted the events of the night, and, but for the evidence of his watch, which still pointed to twenty minutes before twelve, would have been disposed to treat the whole matter as a dream. As it was, he attributed more than half his terrors to the prompting of an over-active and over-wearied brain. For all this, he still felt depressed and uneasy, and so very unwilling to pass another night at Lauterbrunnen, that he made up his mind to proceed that morning to Interlaken. While he was yet loitering over his breakfast, and considering whether he should walk the seven miles of road, or hire a vehicle, a char came rapidly up to the inn door, and a young man jumped out.

"Why, Battisto!" exclaimed my brother, in astonishment, as he came into the room; "what brings you here to-day? Where is Stefano?"

"I have left him at Interlaken, signor," replied the Italian.

Something there was in his voice, something in his face, both strange and startling. "What is the matter?" asked my brother, breathlessly. "He is not ill? No accident has happened?"

Battisto shook his head, glanced furtively up and down the passage, and closed the door.

"Stefano is well, signor; but—but a circumstance has occurred—a circumstance so strange! —Signor, do you believe in spirits?"

"In spirits, Battisto?"

"Ay, signor; for if ever the spirit of any man, dead or living, appealed to human ears, the spirit of Christien came to me last night, at twenty minutes before twelve o'clock."

"At twenty minutes before twelve o'clock!" repeated my brother.

"I was in bed, signor, and Stefano was sleeping in the same room. I had gone up quite warm, and had fallen asleep, full of pleasant thoughts. By-and-by, although I had plenty of bed-clothes, and a rug over me as well, I woke, frozen with cold and scarcely able to breathe. I tried to call to Stefano; but I had no power to utter the slightest sound. I thought my last moment was come. All at once, I heard a sound under the window—a sound which I knew to be Christien's musical box; and it played as it played when we lunched under the fir-trees, except that it was more wild and strange and melancholy and most solemn to hear—awful to hear! Then, signor, it grew fainter and fainter—and then it seemed to float past upon the wind, and die away. When it ceased, my frozen blood grew warm again, and I cried out to Stefano. When I told him what had happened, he declared I had been only dreaming. I made him strike a light, that I might look at my watch. It pointed to twenty minutes before twelve, and had stopped there; and—stranger still—Stefano's watch had done the very same. Now tell me, signor, do you believe that there is any meaning in this, or do you think, as Stefano persists in thinking, that it was all a dream?"

"What is your own conclusion, Battisto?"

"My conclusion, signor, is that some harm has happened to poor Christien on the glacier, and that his spirit came to me last night."

"Battisto, he shall have help if living, or rescue for his poor corpse if dead; for I, too, believe that all is not well."

And with this, my brother told him briefly what had occurred to himself in the night; despatched messengers for the three best guides in Lauterbrunnen; and prepared ropes, ice-hatchets, alpenstocks, and all such matters necessary for a glacier expedition. Hasten as he would, however, it was nearly mid-day before the party started.

Arriving in about half an hour at a place called

Stechelberg, they left the char, in which they had travelled so far, at a châlet, and ascended a steep path in full view of the Breithorn glacier, which rose up to the left, like a battlemented wall of solid ice. The way now lay for some time among pastures and pine-forests. Then they came to a little colony of châlets, called Steinberg, where they filled their water-bottles, got their ropes in readiness, and prepared for the Tschlingel glacier. A few minutes more, and they were on the ice.

At this point, the guides called a halt, and consulted together. One was for striking across the lower glacier towards the left, and reaching the upper glacier by the rocks which bound it on the south. The other two preferred the north, or right side; and this my brother finally took. The sun was now pouring down with almost tropical intensity, and the surface of the ice, which was broken into long treacherous fissures, smooth as glass and blue as the summer sky, was both difficult and dangerous. Silently and cautiously, they went, tied together at intervals of about three yards each: with two guides in front, and the third bringing up the rear. Turning presently to the right, they found themselves at the foot of a steep rock, some forty feet in height, up which they must climb to reach the upper glacier. The only way in which Battisto or my brother could hope to do this, was by the help of a rope steadied from below and above. Two of the guides accordingly clambered up the face of the crag by notches in the surface, and one remained below. The rope was then let down, and my brother prepared to go first. As he planted his foot in the first notch, a smothered cry from Battisto arrested him.

"Santa Maria! Signor! Look yonder!"

My brother looked, and there (he ever afterwards declared), as surely as there is a heaven above us all, he saw Christien Baumann standing in the full sunlight, not a hundred yards distant! Almost in the same moment that my brother recognised him, he was gone. He neither faded, nor sank down, nor moved away; but was simply gone, as if he had never been. Pale as death, Battisto fell upon his knees, and covered his face with his hands. My brother, awe-stricken and speechless, leaned against the rock, and felt that the object of his journey was but too fatally accomplished. As for the guides, they could not conceive what had happened.

"Did you see nothing?" asked my brother and Battisto, both together.

But the men had seen nothing, and the one who had remained below, said, "What should I see but the ice and the sun?"

To this my brother made no other reply than by announcing his intention to have a certain crevasse, from which he had not once removed his eyes since he saw the figure standing on the brink, thoroughly explored before he went a step farther; whereupon the two men came down from the top of the crag, resumed the ropes, and followed my brother, incredulously. At the narrow end of the fissure, he paused, and drove his alpenstock firmly into the ice. It was an unusually long crevasse—at first a mere crack, but widening gradually as it went, and reaching down to unknown depths of dark deep blue, fringed with long pendent icicles, like diamond stalactites. Before they had followed the course of this crevasse for more than ten minutes, the youngest of the guides uttered a hasty exclamation.

"I see something!" cried he. "Something dark, wedged in the teeth of the crevasse, a great way down!"

They all saw it: a mere indistinguishable mass, almost closed over by the ice-walls at their feet. My brother offered a hundred francs to the man who would go down and bring it up. They all hesitated.

"We don't know what it is," said one.

"Perhaps it is only a dead chamois," suggested another.

Their apathy enraged him.

"It is no chamois," he said, angrily. "It is the body of Christien Baumann, native of Kandersteg. And, by Heaven, if you are all too cowardly to make the attempt, I will go down myself!"

The youngest guide threw off his hat and coat, tied a rope about his waist, and took a hatchet in his hand.

"I will go, monsieur," said he; and without another word, suffered himself to be lowered in. My brother turned away. A sickening anxiety came upon him, and presently he heard the dull echo of the hatchet far down in the ice. Then there was a call for another rope, and then—the men all drew aside in silence, and my brother saw the youngest guide standing once more beside the chasm, flushed and trembling, with the body of Christien lying at his feet.

Poor Christien! They made a rough bier with their ropes and alpenstocks, and carried him, with great difficulty, back to Steinberg. There, they got additional help as far as Stechelberg, where they laid him in the char, and so brought him on to Lauterbrunnen. The next day, my brother made it his sad business to precede the body to Kandersteg, and prepare his friends for its arrival. To this day, though all these things happened thirty years ago, he cannot bear to recal Marie's despair, or all the mourning that he innocently brought upon that peaceful valley. Poor Marie has been dead this many a year; and when my brother last passed through the Kander Thal on his way to the Ghemmi, he saw her grave, beside the grave of Christien Baumann, in the village burial-ground.

This is my brother's Ghost Story.

The chairman now announced that the clock declared the teetotum spun out, and that the meeting was dissolved. Yet even then, the young fisherman could not refrain from once more asking his question. This occasioned the Gentlemen King Arthurs, as they got on their hats and great coats, evidently to regard him as a young fisherman who was touched in his head, and some of them even cherished the idea that the captain was his keeper.

As no man dared to awake the mighty Parvis, it was resolved that a heavy member of the society should fall against him as it were by accident, and immediately withdraw to a safe distance. The experiment was so happily accomplished, that Mr. Parvis started to his feet on the best terms with himself, as a light sleeper whose wits never left him, and who could always be broad awake on occasion. Quite an airy jocundity sat upon this respectable man in consequence. And he rallied the briskest member of the fraternity on being "a sleepy-head," with an amount of humour previously supposed to be quite incompatible with his responsible circumstances in life.

Gradually, the society departed into the cold night, and the captain and his young companion were left alone. The captain had so refreshed himself by shaking hands with everybody to an amazing extent, that he was in no hurry to go to bed.

"To-morrow morning," said the captain, "we must find out the lawyer and the clergyman here; they are the people to consult on our business. And I'll be up and out early, and asking questions of everybody I see; thereby propagating at least one of the Institutions of my native country."

As the captain was slapping his leg, the landlord appeared with two small candlesticks.

"Your room," said he, "is at the top of the house. An excellent bed, but you'll hear the wind."

"I've heerd it afore," replied the captain. "Come and make a passage with me, and you shall hear it."

"It's considered to blow, here," said the landlord.

"Weather gets its young strength here," replied the captain; "goes into training for the Atlantic Ocean. Yours are little winds just beginning to feel their way and crawl. Make a voyage with me, and I'll show you a grown-up one out on business. But you haven't told my friend where he lies."

"It's the room at the head of the stairs, before you take the second staircase through the wall," returned the landlord. "You can't mistake it. It's a double-bedded room, because there's no other."

"The room where the seafaring man is?" said the captain.

"The room where the seafaring man is."

"I hope he mayn't finish telling his story in his sleep," remarked the captain. "Shall I turn into the room where the seafaring man is, Alfred?"

"No, Captain Jorgan, why should you? There would be little fear of his waking me, even if he told his whole story out."

"He's in the bed nearest the door," said the landlord. "I've been in to look at him, once, and he's sound enough. Good night, gentlemen."

The captain immediately shook hands with the landlord in quite an enthusiastic manner,

and having performed that national ceremony, as if he had had no opportunity of performing it for a long time, accompanied his young friend up-stairs.

"Something tells me," said the captain as they went, "that Miss Kitty Tregarthen's marriage ain't put off for long, and that we shall light on what we want."

"I hope so. When, do you think?"

"Wa'al, I couldn't just say when, but soon. Here's your room," said the captain, softly opening the door and looking in; "and here's the berth of the seafaring man. I wonder what like he is. He breathes deep; don't he?"

"Sleeping like a child, to judge from the sound," said the young fisherman.

"Dreaming of home, maybe," returned the captain. "Can't see him. Sleeps a deal more wholesomely than Arson Parvis, but a'most as sound; don't he? Good night, fellow-traveller."

"Good night, Captain Jorgan, and many, many thanks!"

"I'll wait till I 'arn 'em, boy, afore I take 'em," returned the captain, clapping him cheerfully on the back. "Pleasant dreams of—you know who!"

When the young fisherman had closed the door, the captain waited a moment or two, listening for any stir on the part of the unknown seafaring man. But, none being audible, the captain pursued the way to his own chamber.

CHAPTER IV.   THE SEAFARING MAN.

WHO was the Seafaring Man? And what might he have to say for himself? He answers those questions in his own words:

I begin by mentioning what happened on my journey, northwards, from Falmouth in Cornwall, to Steepways in Devonshire. I have no occasion to say (being here) that it brought me last night to Lanrean. I had business in hand which was part very serious, and part (as I hoped) very joyful—and this business, you will please to remember, was the cause of my journey.

After landing at Falmouth, I travelled on foot; because of the expense of riding, and because I had anxieties heavy on my mind, and walking was the best way I knew of to lighten them. The first two days of my journey the weather was fine and soft, the wind being mostly light airs from south, and south and by west. On the third day, I took a wrong turning, and had to fetch a long circuit to get right again. Towards evening, while I was still on the road, the wind shifted; and a sea-fog came rolling in on the land. I went on through, what I ask leave to call, the white darkness; keeping the sound of the sea on my left hand for a guide, and feeling those anxieties of mine before mentioned, pulling heavier and heavier at my mind, as the fog thickened and the wet trickled down my face.

It was still early in the evening, when I heard a dog bark, away in the distance, on the right-hand side of me. Following the sound as well as I could, and shouting to the dog, from time to time, to set him barking again, I stumbled up at last against the back of a house; and, hearing voices inside, groped my way round to the door, and knocked on it smartly with the flat of my hand.

The door was opened by a slip-slop young hussey in a torn gown; and the first inquiries I made of her discovered to me that the house was an inn.

Before I could ask more questions, the landlord opened the parlour door of the inn and came out. A clamour of voices, and a fine comforting smell of fire and grog and tobacco, came out, also, along with him.

"The taproom fire's out, says the landlord. "You don't think you would dry more comfortable, like, if you went to bed?" says he, looking hard at me.

"No," says I, looking hard at *him;* "I don't."

Before more words were spoken, a jolly voice hailed us from inside the parlour.

"What's the matter, landlord?" says the jolly voice. "Who is it?"

"A seafaring man, by the looks of him," says the landlord, turning round from me, and speaking into the parlour.

"Let's have the seafaring man in," says the voice. "Let's vote him free of the Club, for this night only."

A lot of other voices thereupon said, "Hear! hear!" in a solemn manner, as if it was church service. After which there was a hammering, as if it was a trunk-maker's shop. After which the landlord took me by the arm; gave me a push into the parlour; and there I was, free of the Club.

The change from the fog outside to the warm room and the shining candles so completely dazed me, that I stood blinking at the company more like an owl than a man. Upon which the company again said, "Hear! hear!" Upon which I returned for answer, "Hear! hear!"—considering those words to mean, in the Club's language, something similar to "How-d'ye-do." The landlord then took me to a round table by the fire, where I got my supper, together with the information that my bedroom, when I wanted it, was number four, up-stairs.

I noticed before I fell to with my knife and fork that the room was full, and that the chairman at the top of the table was the man with the jolly voice, and was seemingly amusing the company by telling them a story. I paid more attention to my supper than to what he was saying; and all I can now report of it is, that his story-telling and my eating and drinking both came to an end together.

"Now," says the chairman, "I have told my story to start you all. Who comes next?" He took up a teetotum, and gave it a spin on the table. When it toppled over, it fell opposite me; upon which the chairman said, "It's your turn next. Order! order! I call on the seafaring man to tell the second story!" He finished the words off with a knock of his hammer; and the Club (having nothing else to

say, as I suppose) tried back, and once again sang out altogether, "Hear! hear!"

"I hope you will please to let me off," I said to the chairman, "for the reason that I have got no story to tell."

"No story to tell?" says he. "A sailor without a story! Who ever heard of such a thing? Nobody!"

"Nobody," says the Club, bursting out altogether at last with a new word, by way of a change.

I can't say I quite relished the chairman's talking of me as if I was before the mast. A man likes his true quality to be known, when he is publicly spoken to among a party of strangers. I made my true quality known to the chairman and company, in these words:

"All men who follow the sea, gentlemen, are sailors," I said. "But there's degrees aboard ship as well as ashore. My rating, if you please, is the rating of a second mate."

"Ay, ay, surely?" says the chairman. "Where did you leave your ship?"

"At the bottom of the sea," I made answer—which was, I am sorry to say, only too true.

"What! you've been wrecked?" says he. "Tell us all about it. A shipwreck-story is just the sort of story we like. Silence there all down the table!—silence for the second mate!"

The Club, upon this, instead of keeping silence, broke out vehemently with another new word, and said, "Chair!" After which every man suddenly held his peace, and looked at me.

I did a very foolish thing. Without stopping to take counsel with myself, I started off at score, and did just what the chairman had bidden me. If they had waited the whole night long for it, I should never have told them the story they wanted from me at first, having all my life been a wretched bad hand at such matters—for the reason, as I take it, that a story is bound to be something which is not true. But when I found the company willing, on a sudden, to put up with nothing better than the account of my shipwreck (which is not a story at all), the unexpected luck of being let off with only telling the truth about myself, was too much of a temptation for me—so I up and told it.

I got on well enough with the storm, and the striking of the vessel, and the strange chance, afterwards, which proved to be the saving of my life—the assembly all listening (to my great surprise) as if they had never heard anything of the sort before. But, when the necessity came next for going further than this, and for telling them what had happened to me *after* the saving of my life—or, to put it plainer, for telling them what place I was cast away on, and what company I was cast away in—the words died straight off on my lips. For this reason—namely—that those particulars of my statement made up just that part of it which I couldn't, and durstn't, let out to strangers—no, not if every man among them had offered me a hundred pounds apiece, on the spot, to do it!

"Go on!" says the chairman. "What happened next? How did you get on shore?"

Feeling what a fool I had been to run myself headlong into a scrape, for want of thinking before I spoke, I now cast about discreetly in my mind for the best means of finishing off-hand without letting out a word to the company concerning those particulars before mentioned. I was some little time before seeing my way to this; keeping the chairman and company, all the while, waiting for an answer. The Club, losing patience in consequence, got from staring hard at me to drumming with their feet, and then to calling out lustily, "Go on! go on! Chair! Order!"—and such like. In the midst of this childish hubbub, I saw my way to what I considered to be rather a neat finish—and got on my legs to ease them all off with it handsomely.

"Hear! hear!" says the Club. "He's going on again at last."

"Gentlemen!" I made answer; "with your permission I will now conclude by wishing you all good night." Saying which words, I gave them a friendly nod, to make things pleasant—and walked straight to the door. It's hardly to be believed—though nevertheless quite true—that these curious men all howled and groaned at me directly, as if I had done them some grievous injury. Thinking I would try to pacify them with their own favourite catch-word, I said, "Hear! hear!" as civilly as might be, whereupon, they all returned for answer, "Oh! oh!" I never belonged to a Club of any kind, myself; and, after what I saw of *that* Club, I don't care if I never do.

My bedroom, when I found my way up to it, was large and airy enough, but not over-clean. There were two beds in it, not over-clean either. Both being empty, I had my choice. One was near the window, and one near the door. I thought the bed near the door looked a trifle the sweetest of the two; and took it.

After falling asleep, it was the grey of the morning before I woke. When I had fairly opened my eyes and shook up my memory into telling me where I was, I made two discoveries. First, that the room was a deal colder in the new morning, than it had been over-night. Second, that the other bed near the window had got some one sleeping in it. Not that I could see the man from where I lay; but I heard his breathing, plain enough. He must have come up into the room, of course, after I had fallen asleep—and he had tumbled himself quietly into bed without disturbing me. There was nothing wonderful in that; and nothing wonderful in the landlord letting the empty bed if he could find a customer for it. I turned, and tried to go to sleep again; but I was out of sorts—out of sorts so badly, that even the breathing of the man in the other bed fretted and worried me. After tumbling and tossing for a quarter of an hour or more, I got up for a change; and walked softly in my stockings, to the window, to look at the morning.

The heavens were brightening into daylight, and the mists were blowing off, past the window, like puffs of smoke. When I got even with the second bed, I stopped to look at the man in it. He lay, sound asleep, turned towards the window; and the end of the counterpane was drawn up over the lower half of his face. Something struck me, on a sudden, in his hair, and his forehead; and, though not an inquisitive man by nature, I stretched out my hand to the end of the counterpane, in spite of myself.

I uncovered his face softly; and there, in the morning light, I saw my brother, Alfred Raybrock.

What I ought to have done, or what other men might have done in my place, I don't know. What I really did, was to drop back a step—to steady myself, with my hand, on the sill of the window—and to stand so, looking at him. Three years ago, I had said good-by to my wife, to my little child, to my old mother, and to brother Alfred here, asleep under my eyes. For all those three years, no news from me had reached them—and the underwriters, as I knew, must have long since reported that the ship I sailed in was lost, and that all hands on board had perished. My heart was heavy when I thought of my kindred at home, and of the weary time they must have waited and sorrowed before they gave me up for dead. Twice I reached out my hand, to wake Alfred, and to ask him about my wife and my child; and twice I drew it back again, in fear of what might happen if he saw me, standing by his bed-head in the grey morning, like Hugh Raybrock risen up from the grave.

I drew my hand back the second time, and waited a minute. In that minute he woke. I had not moved, or spoken a word, or touched him—I had only looked at him longingly. If such things could be, I should say it was my looking that woke him. His eyes, when they opened under mine, passed on a sudden from fast asleep to broad awake. They first settled on my face with a startled look—which passed directly. He lifted himself on his elbow, and opened his lips to speak, but never said a word. His eyes strained and strained into mine; and his face turned all over of a ghastly white. "Alfred!" I said, "don't you know me?" There seemed to be a deadly terror pent up in him, and I thought my voice might set it free. I took fast hold of him by the hands, and spoke again. "Alfred!" I said——

Oh, sirs! where can a man like me find words to tell all that was said and all that was thought between us two brothers? Please to pardon my not saying more of it than I say here. We sat down together, side by side. The poor lad burst out crying—and got vent that way. I kept my hold of his hands, and waited a bit before I spoke to him again. I think I was worst off, now, of the two—no tears came to help *me*—I haven't got my brother's quickness, any way; and my troubles have roughened and hardened me, outside. But, God knows, I felt it keenly; all the more keenly, maybe, because I was slow to show it.

After a little, I put the questions to him which I had been longing to ask, from the time when I first saw his face on the pillow. Had they all given me up at home, for dead (I asked)? Yes; after long, long hoping, one by one they had given me up—my wife (God bless her!) last of all. I meant to ask next if my wife was alive and well; but, try as I might, I could only say "Margaret?"—and look hard in my brother's face. He knew what I meant. Yes (he said), she was living; she was at home; she was in her widow's weeds—poor soul! her widow's weeds! I got on better with my next question about the child. Was it born alive? Yes. Boy or girl? Girl. And living now; and much grown? Living, surely, and grown— poor little thing, what a question to ask!— grown of course, in three years! And mother? Well, mother was a trifle fallen away, and more silent within herself than she used to be— fretting at times; fretting (like my wife) on nights when the sea rose, and the windows shook and shivered in the wind. Thereupon, my brother and I waited a bit again—I with my questions, and he with his answers—and while we waited, I thanked God, inwardly, with all my heart and soul, for bringing me back, living, to wife and kindred, while wife and kindred were living too.

My brother dried the tears off his face; and looked at me a little. Then he turned aside suddenly, as if he remembered something; and stole his hand in a hurry, under the pillow of his bed. Nothing came out from below the pillow but his black neck-handkerchief, which he now unfolded slowly, looking at me, all the while, with something strange in his face that I couldn't make out. "What are you doing?" I asked him. "What are you looking at me like that for?"

Instead of making answer, he took a crumpled morsel of paper out of his neck-handkerchief, opened it carefully, and held it to the light to let me see what it was. Lord in Heaven!—my own writing—the morsel of paper I had committed, long, long since, to the mercy of the deep. Thousands and thousands of miles away, I had trusted that Message to the waters—and here it was now, in my brother's hands! A chilly fear came over me at the seeing it again. Scrap of paper as it was, it looked to my eyes like the ghost of my own past self, gone home before me invisibly over the great wastes of the sea.

My brother pointed down solemnly to the writing.

"Hugh," he said, "were you in your right mind when you wrote those words?"

"Tell me, first," I made answer, "how and when the Message came to you. I can't quiet myself fit to talk till I know that."

He told me how the paper had come to hand —also, how his good friend, the captain, having promised to help him, was then under the same roof with our two selves. But there he stopped. It was not till later in the day that I heard of what had happened (through this dreadful doubt about the money) in the matter of his sweetheart and his marriage.

The knowledge that the Message had reached him by mortal means—on the word of a seaman, I half doubted it when I first set eyes on the paper!—eased me in my mind; and I now did my best to quiet Alfred, in my turn. I told him that I was in my right senses, though sorely troubled, when my hand had written those words. Also, that where the writing was rubbed out, I could tell him for his necessary guidance and mine, what once stood in the empty places. Also, that I knew no more what the real truth might be than he did, till inquiry was made, and the slander on father's good name was dragged boldly into daylight to show itself for what it was worth. Lastly, that all the voyage home, there was one hope and one determination uppermost in my mind—the hope, that I might get safe to England, and find my wife and kindred alive to take me back among them again—the determination, that I would put the doubt about father's five hundred pound to the proof, if ever my feet touched English land once more.

"Come out with me now, Alfred," I said, after winding up as above; "and let me tell you in the quiet of the morning how that Message came to be written and committed to the sea."

We went down stairs softly, and let ourselves out without disturbing any one. The sun was just rising when we left the village and took our way slowly over the cliffs. As soon as the sea began to open on us, I returned to that true story of mine which I had left but half told, the night before—and, this time, I went through with it to the end.

I shipped, as you may remember (were my first words to Alfred), in a second mate's berth, on board the Peruvian, nine hundred tons' burden. We carried an assorted cargo, and we were bound, round the Horn, to Truxillo and Guayaquil, on the western coast of South America. From this last port—namely, Guayaquil —we were to go back to Truxillo, and there to take in another cargo for the return voyage. Those were all the instructions communicated to me when I signed articles with the owners, in London city, three years ago.

After we had been, I think, a week at sea, I heard from the first mate—who had himself heard it from the captain—that the supercargo we were taking with us, on the outward voyage, was to be left at Truxillo, and that another supercargo (also connected with our firm, and latterly employed by them as their foreign agent) was to ship with us at that port, for the voyage home. His name on the captain's instructions was, Mr. Lawrence Clissold. None of us had ever set eyes on him to our knowledge, and none of us knew more about him than what I have told you here.

We had a wonderful voyage out—especially round the Horn. I never before saw such fair weather in that infernal latitude, and I never expect to see the like again. We followed our instructions to the letter; discharging our cargo in fine condition, and returning to Truxillo to load again as directed. At this place, I was so unfortunate as to be seized with the fever of the country, which laid me on my back, while we were in harbour; and which only let me return to my duty after we had been ten days at sea, on the voyage home again. For this reason, the first morning when I was able to get on deck, was also the first time of my setting eyes on our new supercargo, Mr. Lawrence Clissold.

I found him to be a long, lean, wiry man, with some complaint in his eyes which forced him to wear spectacles of blue glass. His age appeared to be fifty-six, or thereabouts; but he might well have been more. There was not above a handful of grey hair, altogether, on his bald head—and, as for the wrinkles at the corners of his eyes and the sides of his mouth, if he could have had a pound apiece in his pocket for every one of them, he might have retired from business from that time forth. Judging by certain signs in his face, and by a suspicious morning-tremble in his hands, I set him down, in my own mind (rightly enough, as it afterwards turned out), for a drinker. In one word, I didn't like the looks of the new supercargo—and, on the first day when I got on deck, I found that he had reasons of his own for paying me back in my own coin, and not liking my looks, either.

"I've been asking the captain about you," were his first words to me in return for my civilly wishing him good morning. "Your name's Raybrock, I hear. Are you any relation to the late Hugh Raybrock, of Barnstaple, Devonshire?"

"Rather a near relation," I made answer. "I am the late Hugh Raybrock's eldest son."

There was no telling how his eyes looked, because they were hidden by his blue spectacles —but I saw him wince at the mouth, when I gave him that reply.

"Your father ended by failing in business, didn't he?" was the next question the supercargo put to me.

"Who told you he failed?" I asked, sharply enough.

"Oh! I heard it," says Mr. Lawrence Clissold, both looking and speaking as if he was glad to have heard it, and he hoped it was true.

"Whoever told you my father failed in business, told you a lie," I said. "His business fell off towards the last years of his life—I don't deny it. But every creditor he had was honestly paid at his death, without so much as touching the provision left for his widow and children. Please to mention that, next time you hear it reported that my father failed in business."

Mr. Clissold grinned to himself—and I lost my temper.

"I'll tell you what," I said to him, "I don't like your laughing to yourself, when I ask you to do justice to my father's memory—and, what is more, I didn't like the way you mentioned that report of his failing in business, just now. You looked as if you hoped it was true."

"Perhaps I did," says Mr. Clissold, coolly. "Shall I tell you why? When I was a young man, I was unlucky enough to owe your father some money. He was a merciless creditor;

and he threatened me with a prison if the debt remained unpaid on the day when it was due. I have never forgotten that circumstance; and I should certainly not have been sorry if your father's creditors had given him a lesson in forbearance, by treating him as harshly as he once treated me."

"My father had a right to ask for his own," I broke out. "If you owed him the money and didn't pay it——"

"I never told you I didn't pay it," says Mr. Clissold, as coolly as ever.

"Well, if you did pay it," I put in, "then, you didn't go to prison—and you have no cause of complaint now. My father wronged nobody; and I won't believe he ever wronged you. He was a just man in all his dealings; and whoever tells me to the contrary——!"

"That will do," says Mr. Clissold, backing away to the cabin stairs. "You seem to have not quite got over your fever yet. I'll leave you to air yourself in the sea-breezes, Mr. Second Mate; and I'll receive your excuses when you are cool enough to make them."

"It is a son's business to defend his father's character," I answered; "and, cool or hot, I'll leave the ship sooner than ask your pardon for doing my duty!"

"You will leave the ship," says the supercargo, quietly going down into the cabin. "You will leave at the next port, if I have any interest with the captain."

That was how Mr. Clissold and I scraped acquaintance on the first day when we met together! And as we began, so we went on to the end. But, though he persecuted me in almost every other way, he did not anger me again about father's affairs: he seemed to have dropped talking of them at once and for ever. On my side I nevertheless bore in mind what he had said to me, and determined, if I got home safe, to go to the lawyer at Barnstaple who keeps father's old books and letters for us, and see what information they might give on the subject of Mr. Lawrence Clissold. I, myself, had never heard his name mentioned at home—father (as you know, Alfred) being always close about business-matters, and mother never troubling him with idle questions about his affairs. But it was likely enough that he and Mr. Clissold might have been concerned in money-matters, in past years, and that Mr. Clissold might have tried to cheat him, and failed. I rather hoped it might prove to be so—for the truth is, the supercargo provoked me past all endurance; and I hated him as heartily as he hated me.

All this while the ship was making such a speedy voyage down the coast, that we began to think we were carrying back with us the fine weather we had brought out. But, on nearing Cape Horn, the signs and tokens appeared which told us that our run of luck was at an end. Down went the barometer, lower and lower; and up got the wind, in the northerly quarter, higher and higher. This happened towards nightfall—and at daybreak next day, we found ourselves forced to lay-to. It blew all that day and all that night; towards noon the next day, it lulled a little, and we made sail again. But at sunset, the heavens grew blacker than ever; and the wind returned upon us with double and treble fury. The Peruvian was a fine stout roomy ship, but the unhandiest vessel at laying-to I ever sailed in. After taking tons of water on board and losing our best boat, we had nothing left for it but to turn tail, and scud for our lives. For the next three days and nights we ran before the wind. The gale moderated more than once in that time; but there was such a sea on, that we durstn't heave the ship to. From the beginning of the gale none of us officers had a chance of taking any observations. We only knew that the wind was driving us as hard as we could go in a southerly direction, and that we were by this time hundreds of miles out of the ordinary course of ships in doubling the Cape.

On the third night—or rather, I should say, early on the fourth morning—I went below, dead beat, to get a little rest, leaving the vessel in charge of the captain and the first mate. The night was then pitch-black—it was raining, hailing, and sleeting, all at once—and the Peruvian was wallowing in the frightful seas, as if she meant to roll the masts out of her. I tumbled into bed the instant my wet oilskins were off my back, and slept as only a man can who lays himself down dead beat.

I was woke—how long afterwards I don't know—by being pitched clean out of my berth on to the cabin floor; and, at the same moment, I heard the crash of the ship's timbers, forward, which told me it was all over with us.

Though bruised and shaken by my fall, I was on deck directly. Before I had taken two steps forward, the Peruvian forged ahead on the send of the sea, swung round a little, and struck heavily at the bows for the second time. The shrouds of the foremast cracked one after another, like pistol-shots; and the mast went overboard. I next felt our people go tearing past me, in the black darkness, to the lee-side of the vessel; and I knew that, in their last extremity, they were taking to the boats. I say I *felt* them go past me, because the roaring of the sea and the howling of the wind deafened me, on deck, as completely as the darkness blinded me. I myself no more believed the boats would live in the sea, than I believed the ship would hold together on the reef—but, as the rest were running the risk, I made up my mind to run it with them.

But before I followed the crew to leeward, I went below again for a minute—not to save money or clothes, for, with death staring me in the face, neither were of any account, now—but to get my little writing-case which mother had given me at parting. A curl of Margaret's hair was in the pocket inside it, with all the letters she had sent me when I had been away on other voyages. If I saved anything I was resolved to save this—and if I died, I would die with it about me.

My locker was jammed with the wrenching of the ship, and had to be broken open. I was, maybe, longer over this job than I myself supposed. At any rate, when I got on deck again with my case in my breast, it was useless calling, and useless groping about. The largest of the two boats, when I felt for it, was gone; and every soul on board was beyond a doubt gone with her.

Before I had time to think, I was thrown off my feet, by another sea coming on board, and a great heave of the vessel, which drove her farther over the reef, and canted the after-part of her up like the roof of a house. In that position the stern stuck, wedged fast into the rocks beneath, while the fore-part of the ship was all to pieces and down under water. If the after-part kept the place it was now jammed in, till daylight, there might be a chance—but if the sea wrenched it out from between the rocks, there was an end of me. After straining my eyes to discover if there was land beyond the reef, and seeing nothing but the flash of the breakers, like white fire in the darkness, I crawled below again to the shelter of the cabin stairs, and waited for death or daylight.

As the morning hours wore on, the weather moderated again; and the after-part of the vessel, though shaken often, was not shaken out of its place. A little before dawn, the winds and the waves, though fierce enough still, allowed me, at last, to hear something besides themselves. What I did hear, crouched up in my dark corner, was a heavy thumping and grinding, every now and then, against the side of the ship to windward. Day broke soon afterwards; and, when I climbed to the deck, I clawed my way up to windward first, to see what the noise was caused by.

My first look over the bulwark showed me that it was caused by the boat which my unfortunate brother-officers and the crew had launched and gone away in when the ship struck. The boat was bottom upwards, thumping against the ship's side on the lift of the sea. I wanted no second look at it to tell me that every mother's son of them was drowned.

The main and mizen masts still stood. I got into the mizen rigging, to look out next to leeward—and there, in the blessed daylight, I saw a low, green, rocky little island, lying away beyond the reef, barely a mile distant from the ship! My life began to look of some small value to me again, when I saw land. I got higher up in the rigging to note how the current set, and where there might be a passage through the reef. The ship had driven over the rocks through the worst of the surf, and the sea between myself and the island, though angry and broken in places, was not too high for a lost man like me to venture on—provided I could launch the last, and smallest, boat still left in the vessel. I noted carefully the likeliest-looking channel for trying the experiment, and then got down on deck again to see what I could do, first of all, with the boat.

At the moment when my feet touched the

deck, I heard a dull knocking and banging just under them, in the region of the cabin. When the sound first reached my ears, I got such a shock of surprise that I could neither move nor speak. It had never yet crossed my mind that a single soul was left in the vessel besides myself—but now, there was something in the knocking noise which started the hope in me that I was not alone. I shook myself up, and got down below directly.

The noise came from inside one of the sleeping berths, on the far side of the main cabin; the door of which was jammed, no doubt, just as my locker had been jammed, by the wrenching of the ship. "Who's there?" I called out. A faint, muffled kind of voice answered something through the air-grating in the upper part of the door. I got up on the overthrown cabin furniture; and, looking in through the trellis-work of the grating, found myself face to face with the blue spectacles of Mr. Lawrence Clissold, looking out!

God forgive me for thinking it—but there was not a man in the vessel I wouldn't sooner have found alive in her than Mr. Clissold! Of all that ship's company, we two, who were least friendly together, were the only two saved.

I had a better chance of breaking out the jammed door from the main cabin, than he had from the berth inside; and in less than five minutes he was set free. I had smelt spirits already through the air-grating—and now, when he and I stood face to face, I saw what the smell meant. There was an open case of spirits by the bedside—two of the bottles out of it were lying broken on the floor—and Mr. Clissold was drunk.

"What's the matter with the ship?" says he, looking fierce, and speaking thick.

"You shall see for yourself," says I. With which words I took hold of him, and pulled him after me up the cabin stairs. I reckoned on the sight that would meet him, when he first looked over the deck, to sober his drunken brains—and I reckoned right: he fell on his knees, stock-still and speechless as if he was turned to stone.

I lashed him up safe to the cabin rail, and left it to the air to bring him round. He had, likely enough, been drinking in the sleeping berth for days together—for none of us, as I now remembered, had seen him since the gale set in—and even if he had had sense enough to try to get out, or to call for help, when the ship struck, he would not have made himself heard in the noise and confusion of that awful time. But for the lull in the weather, I should not have heard him myself, when he attempted to get free in the morning. Enemy of mine as he was, he had a pair of arms—and he was worth untold gold, in my situation, for that reason. With the help I could make him give me, there was no doubt now about launching the boat. In half an hour I had the means ready for trying the experiment; and Mr. Clissold was sober enough to see that his life depended on his doing what I told him.

The sky looked angry still—there was no opening anywhere—and the clouds were slowly banking up again to windward. The supercargo knew what I meant when I pointed that way, and worked with a will when I gave him the word. I had previously stowed away in the boat such stores of meat, biscuit, and fresh water as I could readily lay hands on; together with a compass, a lantern, a few candles, and some boxes of matches in my pocket, to kindle light and fire with. At the last moment, I thought of a gun and some powder and shot. The powder and shot I found, and an old flint pocket-pistol in the captain's cabin—with which, for fear of wasting precious time, I was forced to be content. The pistol lay on the top of the medicine-chest—and I took that also, finding it handy, and not knowing but what it might be of use. Having made these preparations, we launched the boat, down the steep of the deck, into the water over the forward part of the ship which was sunk. I took the oars, ordering Mr. Clissold to sit still in the stern-sheets—and pulled for the island.

It was neck or nothing with us more than once, before we were two hundred yards from the ship. Luckily, the supercargo was used to boats; and muddled as he still was, he had sense enough to sit quiet. We found our way into the smooth channel which I had noted from the mizen rigging—after which, it was easy enough to get ashore.

We landed on a little sandy creek. From the time of our leaving the ship, the supercargo had not spoken a word to me, nor I to him. I now told him to lend a hand in getting the stores out of the boat, and in helping me to carry them to the first sheltered place we could find in shore on the island. He shook himself up with a sulky look at me, and did as I had bidden him. We found a little dip or dell in the ground, after getting up the low sides of the island, which was sheltered to windward—and here I left him to stow away the stores, while I walked farther on, to survey the place.

According to the hasty judgment I formed at the time, the island was not a mile across, and not much more than three miles round. I noted nothing in the way of food but a few wild roots and vegetables, growing in ragged patches amidst the thick scrub which covered the place. There was not a tree on it anywhere; nor any living creatures; nor any signs of fresh water that I could see. Standing on the highest ground, I looked about anxiously for other islands that might be inhabited; there were none visible—at least none in the hazy state of the heavens that morning. When I fairly discovered what a desert the place was; when I remembered how far it lay out of the track of ships; and when I thought of the small store of provisions which we had brought with us, the doubt lest we might only have changed the chance of death by drowning for the chance of death by starvation was so strong in me, that I determined to go back to the boat, with the desperate notion of making another trip to the vessel for water and food. I say desperate, because the clouds to windward were banking up blacker and higher every minute, the wind was freshening already, and there was every sign of the storm coming on again wilder and fiercer than ever.

Mr. Clissold, when I passed him on my way back to the beach, had got the stores pretty tidy, covered with the tarpaulin which I had thrown over them in the bottom of the boat. Just as I looked down at him in the hollow, I saw him take a bottle of spirits out of the pocket of his pilot-coat. He must have stowed the bottle away there, as I suppose, while I was breaking open the door of his berth. "You'll be drowned, and I shall have double allowance to live upon here," was all he said to me, when he heard I was going back to the ship. "Yes! and die, in your turn, when you've got through it," says I, going away to the boat. It's shocking to think of now—but we couldn't be civil to each other, even on the first day when we were wrecked together!

Having previously stripped to my trousers, in case of accident, I now pulled out. On getting from the channel into the broken water again, I looked over my shoulder to windward, and saw that I was too late. It was coming!—the ship was hidden already in the horrible haze of it. I got the boat's head round to pull back—and I did pull back, just inside the opening in the reef which made the mouth of the channel—when the storm came down on me like death and judgment. The boat filled in an instant; and I was tossed head over heels into the water. The sea, which burst into raging surf upon the rocks on either side, rushed in one great roller up the deep channel between them, and took me with it. If the undertow, afterwards, had lasted for half a minute, I should have been carried into the white water, and lost. But a second roller followed the first, almost on the instant, and swept me right up on the beach. I had just strength enough to dig my arms and legs well into the wet sand; and though I was taken back with the backward shift of it, I was not taken into deep water again. Before the third roller came, I was out of its reach, and was down in a sort of swoon, on the dry sand.

When I got back to the hollow, in shore, where I had left my clothes under shelter with the stores, I found Mr. Clissold snugly crouched up, in the driest place, with the tarpaulin to cover him. "Oh!" says he, in a state of great surprise, "you're not drowned?" "No," says I; "you won't get your double allowance, after all." "How much shall I get?" says he, rousing up and looking anxious. "Your fair half share of what is here," I answered him. "And how long will that last me?" says he. "The food, if you have sense enough to eke it out with what you may find in this miserable place, barely three weeks," says I; "and the water (if you ever drink any) about a fortnight." At hearing that, he took the bottle out of his pocket again, and put it to his lips. "I'm cold to the bones," says I, frowning at him for a drop. "And I'm warm to the marrow," says he, chuckling, and

handing me the bottle empty. I pitched it away at once—or the temptation to break it over his head might have been too much for me—I pitched it away, and looked into the medicine-chest, to see if there was a drop of peppermint, or anything comforting of that sort, inside. Only three physic bottles were left in it, all three being neatly tied over with oilskin. One of them held a strong white liquor, smelling like hartshorn. The other two were filled with stuff in powder, having the names in printed gibberish, pasted outside. On looking a little closer, I found, under some broken divisions of the chest, a small flask covered with wicker-work. "Ginger-Brandy" was written with pen and ink on the wicker-work, and the flask was full! I think that blessed discovery saved me from shivering myself to pieces. After a pull at the flask which made a new man of me, I put it away in my inside breast-pocket; Mr. Clissold watching me with greedy eyes, but saying nothing.

All this while, the rain was rushing, the wind roaring, and the sea crashing, as if Noah's Flood had come again. I sat close against the super-cargo, because he was in the driest place; and pulled my fair share of the tarpaulin away from him, whether he liked it or not. He by no means liked it; being in that sort of half-drunken, half-sober state (after finishing his bottle), in which a man's temper is most easily upset by trifles. The upset of *his* temper showed itself in the way of small aggravations—of which I took no notice, till he suddenly bethought himself of angering me by going back again to that dispute about father, which had bred ill-blood between us, on the day when we first saw each other. If he had been a younger man, I am afraid I should have stopped him by a punch on the head. As it was, considering his age and the shame of this quarrelling betwixt us when we were both cast away together, I only warned him that I *might* punch his head, if he went on. It did just as well—and I'm glad now to think that it did.

We were huddled so close together, that when he coiled himself up to sleep (with a growl), and when he did go to sleep (with a grunt), he growled and grunted into my ear. His rest, like the rest of all the regular drunkards I have ever met with, was broken. He ground his teeth, and talked in his sleep. Among the words he mumbled to himself, I heard as plain as could be father's name. This vexed, but did not surprise me, seeing that he had been talking of father before he dropped off. But when I made out next, among his mutterings and mumblings, the words "five hundred pound," spoken over and over again, with father's name, now before, now after, now mixed in along with them, I got curious, and listened for more. My listening (and, serve me right, you will say) came to nothing: he certainly talked on, but I couldn't make out a word more that he said.

When he woke up, I told him plainly he had been talking in his sleep—and mightily taken aback he looked when he first heard it. "What about?" says he. I made answer, "My father, and five hundred pound; and how do you come to couple them together, I should like to know?" "I couldn't have coupled them," says he, in a great hurry—"what do I know about it? I don't believe a man like your father ever had such a sum of money as that, in all his life." "Don't you?" says I, feeling the aggravation of him, in spite of myself; "I can just tell you my father had such a sum when he was no older a man than I am—and saved it—and left it for a provision, in his will, to my mother; how came a stranger like you to be talking of it in your sleep?" At hearing this, he went about on the other tack directly. "Was that all your father left, after his debts were paid?" says he. "Are you very curious to know?" says I. He took no notice—he only persisted with his question. "Was it just five hundred pound, no more and no less?" says he. "Suppose it was," says I; "what then?" "Oh, nothing?" says he, and turns sharp round from me, and chuckles to himself. "You're drunk!" says I. "Yes," says he; "that's it—stick to that—I'm drunk" —and he chuckles again. Try as I might, and threaten as I might, not another word on the matter of the five hundred pound could I get from him. I bore it well in mind, though, for all that—it being one of my slow ways, not easily to forget anything that has once surprised me, and not to give up returning to it over and over again, as time and occasion may serve for the purpose.

The hours wore on, and the storm raged on. We had our half rations of food, when hunger took us (I being much the hungrier of the two); and slept, and grumbled, and quarrelled the weary time out somehow. Towards dusk the wind lessened; and, when I got up, out of the hollow to look out, there was a faint watery break in the western heavens. At times, through the watches of the long night, the stars showed in patches for a little while, through the rents that opened and closed by fits in the black sky. When I fell asleep towards the dawning, the wind had fallen to a moan, though the sea, slower to go down, sounded as loud as ever. From what I could make of the weather, the storm had, by that time, as good as blown itself out.

I had been wise enough (knowing who was near me) to lay myself down, whenever I slept, on the side of me which was next to the flask of ginger-brandy. When I woke at sunrise, it was the supercargo's hand that roused me up, trying to steal my flask while I was asleep. I rolled him over headlong among the stores—out of which I had the humanity to pull him again, with my own hands.

"I'll tell you what," says I, "if us two keep company any longer, we shan't get on smoothly together. You're the oldest man—and you stop here, where we know there is shelter. We will divide the stores fairly, and I'll go and shift for myself at the other end of the island. Do you agree to that?"

"Yes," says he; "and the sooner the better."

I left him for a minute, and went away to look out on the reef that had wrecked us. The splinters of the Peruvian, scattered broadcast over the beach, or tossing up and down darkly, far out in the white surf, were all that remained to tell of the ship. I don't deny that my heart sank, when I looked at the place where she struck, and saw nothing before me but sea and sky.

But what was the use of standing and looking? It was a deal better to rouse myself by doing something. I returned to Mr. Clissold— and then and there divided the stores into two equal parts, including everything down to the matches in my pocket. Of these parts I gave him first choice. I also left him the whole of the tarpaulin to himself—keeping in my own possession the medicine-chest, and the pistol; which last I loaded with powder and shot, in case any sea-birds might fly within reach. When the division was made, and when I had moved my part out of his way and out of his sight, I thought it uncivil to bear malice any longer, now that we had agreed to separate. We were cast away on a desert island, and we had death, as well as I could see, within about three weeks' hail of us—but that was no reason for not making things reasonably pleasant as long as we could. I was some time (in consequence of my natural slowness where matters of seafaring duty don't happen to be concerned) before I came to this conclusion. When I did come to it, I acted on it.

"Shake hands, before parting," I said, suiting the action to the word.

"No!" says he; "I don't like you."

"Please yourself," says I—and so we parted.

Turning my back on the west, which was his territory according to agreement, I walked away towards the south-east, where the sides of the island rose highest. Here I found a sort of half rift, half cavern, in the rocky banks, which looked as likely a place as any other—and to this refuge I moved my share of the stores. I thatched it over as well as I could with scrub, and heaped up some loose stones at the mouth of it. At home in England, I should have been ashamed to put my dog in such a place—but when a man believes his days to be numbered, he is not over-particular about his lodgings, and I was not over-particular about mine.

When my work was done, the heavens were fair, the sun was shining, and it was long past noon. I went up again to the high ground, to see what I could make out in the new clearness of the air. North, east, and west there was nothing but sea and sky—but, south, I now saw land. It was high, and looked to be a matter of seven or eight miles off. Island, or not, it must have been of a good size for me to see it as I did. Known or not known to mariners, it was certainly big enough to have living creatures on it—animals or men, or both. If I had not lost the boat in my second attempt to reach the vessel, we might have easily got to it. But situated as we were now, with no wood to make a boat of but the scattered splinters from the ship, and with no tools to use even that much, there might just as well have been no land in sight at all, so far as we were concerned. The poor hope of a ship coming our road, was still the only hope left. To give us all the little chance we might get that way, I now looked about on the beach for the longest morsel of a wrecked spar that I could find; planted it on the high ground; and rigged up to it the one shirt I had on my back for a signal. While coming and going on this job, I noted with great joy that rain water enough lay in the hollows of the rocks above the sea line, to save our small store of fresh water for a week at least. Thinking it only fair to the supercargo to let him know what I had found out, I went to his territories, after setting up the morsel of a spar, and discreetly shouted my news down to him without showing myself. "Keep to your own side!" was all the thanks I got for this piece of civility. I went back to my own side immediately, and crawled into my little cavern, quite content to be alone. On that first night, strange as it seems now, I once or twice nearly caught myself feeling happy at the thought of being rid of Mr. Lawrence Clissold.

According to my calculations—which were made by tying a fresh knot every morning in a piece of marline—we two men were just a week, each on his own side of the island, without seeing or communicating, anyhow, with one another. The first half of the week, I had enough to do with cudgelling my brains for a means of helping ourselves, to keep my mind steady.

I thought first of picking up all the longest bits of spars that had been cast ashore, lashing them together with ropes twisted out of the long grass on the island, and trusting to raft-navigation to get to that high land away in the south. But when I looked among the spars, there were not half a dozen of them left whole enough for the purpose. And even if there had been more, the short allowance of food would not have given me time sufficient, or strength sufficient, to gather the grass, to twist it into ropes, and to lash a raft together big enough and strong enough for us two men. There was nothing to be done, but to give up this notion—and I gave it up. The next chance I thought of was to keep a fire burning on the shore every night, with the wood of the wreck, in case vessels at sea might notice it, on one side—or the people of the high land in the south (if the distance was not too great) might notice it, on the other. There was sense in this notion, and it could be turned to account the moment the wood was dry enough to burn. The wood got dry enough before the week was out. Whether it was the end of the stormy season in those latitudes, or whether it was only the shifting of the wind to the west, I don't know—but now, day after day, the heavens were clear and the sun shone scorching hot. The scrub on the island (which was of no great account)

dried up—but the fresh water in the hollows of the rocks (which was, on the other hand, a serious business) dried up too. Troubles seldom come alone ; and on the day when I made this discovery, I also found out that I had calculated wrong about the food. Eke it out as I might, with scurvy grass and roots, there would not be above eight days more of it left when the first week was past—and, as for the fresh water, half a pint a day, unless more rain fell, would leave me at the end of my store, as nearly as I could guess, about the same time.

This was a bad look-out—but I don't think the prospect of it upset me in my mind, so much as the having nothing to do. Except for the gathering of the wood, and the lighting of the signal-fire, every night, I had no work at all, towards the end of the week, to keep me steady. I checked myself in thinking much about home, for fear of losing heart, and not holding out to the last, as became a man. For the same reasons I likewise kept my mind from raising hopes of help in me which were not likely to come true. What else was there to think about? Nothing but the man on the other side of the island—and be hanged to him !

I thought about those words I heard him say in his sleep; I thought about how he was getting on by himself; how he liked nothing but water to drink, and little enough of that ; how he was eking out his food; whether he slept much or not ; whether he saw the smoke of my fire at night, or not ; whether he held up better or worse than I did; whether he would be glad to see me, if I went to him to make it up ; whether he or I would die first; whether if it was me, he would do for me, what I would have done for him—namely, bury him, with the last strength I had left. All these things, and lots more, kept coming and going in my mind, till I could stand it no longer. On the morning of the eighth day, I roused up to go to his territories, feeling it would do me good to see him and hear him, even if we quarrelled again the instant we set eyes on each other.

I climbed up to the grassy ground—and, when I got there, what should I see but the supercargo himself, coming to my territories, and wandering up and down in the scrub through not knowing where to find them !

It almost knocked me over, when we met, the man was changed so. He looked eighty years old; the little flesh he had on his miserable face hung baggy; his blue spectacles had dropped down on his nose, and his eyes showed over them wild and red-rimmed ; his lips were black, his legs staggered under him. He came up to me with his eyes all of a glare, and put both his hands on my breast, just over the pocket in which I kept that flask of ginger-brandy which he had tried to steal from me.

"Have you got any of it left?" says he, in a whisper.

"About two mouthfuls," says I.

"Give us one of them, for God's sake," says he.

Giving him one of those mouthfuls was just

about equal to giving him a day of my life. In the ease of a man I liked, I would not have thought twice about giving it. In the case of Mr. Clissold, I did think twice. I would have been a better Christian, if I could—but just then, I couldn't.

He thought I was going to say, No. His eyes got eunning directly. He reached his hands to my shoulders, and whispered these words in my ear:

"I'll tell you what I know about the five hundred pound, if you'll give me a drop."

I determined to give it to him, and pulled out the flask. I took his hand, and poured the drop into the hollow of it, and held it for a moment.

"Tell me first," I said, "and drink afterwards."

He looked all round him, as if he thought there were people on the island to hear us. "Hush!" he said; "let's whisper about it." The next question and answer that passed between us, was louder than before on my side, and softer than ever on his. This was the question:

"What do you know about the five hundred pound?"

And this was the answer:

"It's *Stolen Money!*"

My hand dropped away from his, as if he had shot me. He instantly fastened on the drop of liquor in the hollow of his hand, like a hungry wild beast on a bone, and then looked up for more. Something in my face (God knows what) seemed suddenly to frighten him out of his life. Before I could stir a step, or get a word out, down he dropped on his knees, whining and whimpering in the high grass at my feet.

"Don't kill me!" says he; "I'm dying—I'll think of my poor soul. I'll repent while there's time——"

Beginning in that way, he maundered awfully, grovelling down in the grass; asking me every other minute for "a drop more, and a drop more;" and talking as if he thought we were both in England. Out of his wanderings, his beseechings for another drop, and his miserable beggar's-petitions for his "poor soul," I gathered together these words—the same which I wrote down on the morsel of paper, and of which nine parts out of ten are now rubbed off!

The first I made out—though not the first he said—was that some one, whom he spoke of as "the old man," was alive; and "Lanrean" was the place he lived in. I was to go there, and ask, among the old men, for "Tregarthen——"

(At the mention by me of the name of Tregarthen, my brother, to my great surprise, stopped me with a start; made me say the name over more than once; and then, for the first time, told me of the trouble about his sweetheart and his marriage. We waited a little to talk that matter over; after which, I went on again with my story, in these words:)

Well, as I made out from Clissold's wanderings, I was to go to Lanrean, to ask among the old men for Tregarthen, and to say to Tregarthen, "Clissold was the man. Clissold bore

no malice: Clissold repented like a Christian, for the sake of his poor soul." No! I was to say something else to Tregarthen. I was to say, "Look among the books; look at the leaf you know of, and see for yourself it's not the right leaf to be there." No! I was to say something else to Tregarthen. I was to say, "The right leaf is hidden, not burnt. Clissold had time for everything else, but no time to burn that leaf. Tregarthen came in when he had got the candle lit to burn it. There was just time to let it drop from under his hand into the great crack in the desk, and then he was ordered abroad by the House, and there was no chance of doing more." No! I was to say none of these things to Tregarthen. Only this, instead:—"Look in Clissold's Desk—and, if you blame anybody, blame miser Raybroek for driving him to it." And, oh, another drop—for the Lord's sake, give him another drop!

So he went on, over and over again, till I found voice enough to speak, and stop him.

"Get up, and go!" I said to the miserable wretch. "Get back to your own side of the island, or I may do you a mischief, in spite of my own self."

"Give me the other drop, and I will"—was all the answer I could get from him.

I threw him the flask. He pounced upon it with a howl. I turned my back—for I could look at him no longer—and climbed down again to my cavern on the beach.

I sat down alone on the sand, and tried to quiet myself fit to think about what I had heard. That father could ever have wilfully done anything unbecoming his character as an honest man, was what I wouldn't believe, in the first place. And that the wretched brute I had just parted from was in his right senses, was what I wouldn't believe, in the second place. What I had myself seen of drinkers, at sea and ashore, helped me to understand the condition into which he had fallen. I knew that when a man who has been a drunkard for years, is suddenly cut off his drink, he drops to pieces like, body and mind, for the want of it. I had also heard ship-doctors talk, by some name of their own, of a drink-madness, which we ignorant men call the Horrors. And I made it out, easy enough, that I had seen the supereargo in the first of these conditions; and that if we both lived long enough without help coming to us, I might soon see him in the second. But when I tried to get farther, and settle how much of what I had heard was wanderings and how much truth, and what it meant if any of it was truth, my slowness got into my way again; and where a quicker man might have made up his mind in an hour or two, I was all day, in sore distress, making up mine. The upshot of what I settled with myself was, in two words, this:—Having mother's writing-case handy about me, I determined first to set down for my own self's reminder, all that I had heard. Second, to clear the matter up if ever I got back to England alive; and, if wrong had been done to that old man, or to anybody else, in father's name (without father's knowledge), to make restoration for his sake.

All that day I neither saw nor heard more of the supercargo. I passed a miserable night of it, after writing my memorandum, fighting with my loneliness and my own thoughts. The remembrance of those words in father's will, saying that the five hundred pound was money which he had once run a risk with, kept putting into my mind suspicions I was ashamed of. When daylight came, I almost felt as if I was going to have the Horrors too, and got up to walk them off, if possible, in the morning air.

I kept on the northern side of the island, walking backwards and forwards for an hour or more. Then I returned to my cavern; and the first thing I saw, on getting near it, was other footsteps than mine marked on the sand. I suspected at once that the supercargo had been lurking about watching me, instead of going back to his own side; and that, in my absence, he had been at his thieving tricks again.

The stores were what I looked at first. The food he had not touched; but the water he had either drunk or wasted—there was not half a pint of it left. The medicine-chest was open, and the bottle with the hartshorn was gone. When I looked next for the pistol, which I had loaded with powder and shot for the chance of bird-shooting that never came, the pistol was gone too. After making this last discovery, there was but one thing to be done—namely—to find out where he was, and to take the pistol away from him.

I set off to search first on the western side. It was a beautiful clear, calm, sunshiny morning; and as I crossed the island, looking out on my left hand and my right, I stopped on a sudden, with my heart in my mouth, as the saying is. Something caught my eye, far out at sea, in the north-west. I looked again—and there, as true as the heavens above me, I saw a ship, with the sunlight on her topsails, hull down, on the water-line in the offing!

All thought of the errand I was bent on, went out of my mind in an instant. I ran as fast as my weak legs would carry me to the northern beach; gathered up the broken wood which was still lying there plentifully, and, with the help of the dry scrub, lit the largest fire I had made yet. This was the only signal it was in my power to make that there were men on the island. The fire, in the bright daylight, would never be visible to the ship; but the smoke curling up from it, in the clear sky, might be seen, if they had a look-out at the mast-head.

While I was still feeding the fire, and so wrapped up in doing it, that I had neither eyes nor ears for anything else, I heard the supercargo's voice on a sudden at my back. He had stolen on me along the sand. When I faced him, he was swinging his arms about in the air, and saying to himself over and over again, "I see the ship! I see the ship!"

After a little, he came close up to me. By the look of him, he had been drinking the hartshorn, and it had strung him up a bit, body and mind, for the time. He kept his right hand behind him, as if he was hiding something. I suspected that "something" to be the pistol I was in search of.

"Will the ship come here?" says he.

"Yes, if they see the smoke," says I, keeping my eye on him.

He waited a bit, frowning suspiciously, and looking hard at me all the time.

"What did I say to you yesterday?" he asked.

"What I have got written down here," I made answer, smacking my hand over the writing-case in my breast-pocket; "and what I mean to put to the proof, if the ship sees us and we get back to England."

He whipped his right hand round from behind him, like lightning; and snapped the pistol at me. It missed fire. I wrenched it from him in a moment, and was just within one hair's breadth of knocking him on the head with the butt-end, afterwards. I lifted my hand—then thought better, and dropped it again.

"No," says I, fixing my eyes on him steadily; "I'll wait till the ship finds us."

He slunk away from me; and, as he slunk, looked hard into the fire. He stopped a minute so, thinking to himself—then he looked back at me again, with some mad mischief in him, that twinkled through his blue spectacles, and grinned on his dry black lips.

"The ship shall never find *you*," he said. With which words, he turned himself about towards his own side of the island, and left me.

He only meant that saying to be a threat—but, bird of ill-omen that he was, it turned out as good as a prophecy! All my hard work with the fire proved work in vain; all hope was quenched in me, long before the embers I had set light to were burnt out. Whether the smoke was seen or not from the vessel, is more than I can tell. I only know that she filled away on the other tack, not ten minutes after the supercargo left me. In less than an hour's time the last glimpse of the bright topsails had vanished out of view.

I went back to my cavern—which was now likelier than ever to be my grave as well. In that hot climate, with all the moisture on the island dried up, with not quite so much as a tumbler-full of fresh water left, with my strength wasted by living on half-rations of food—two days more at most would see me out. It was hard enough for a man at my age, with all that I had left at home to make life precious, to die such a death as was now before me. It was harder still to have the sting of death sharpened —as I felt it, then—by what had just happened between the supercargo and myself. There was no hope, now, that his wanderings, the day before, had more falsehood than truth in them. The secret he had let out was plainly true enough and serious enough to have scared him into attempting my life, rather than let me keep possession of it, when there was a chance of the ship rescuing us. That secret had father's good name mixed up with it—and here was I, instead of clearing the villanous darkness from off of it, carrying it with me, black as ever, into my grave.

It was out of the horror I felt at doing that, and out of the yearning of my heart towards you, Alfred, when I thought of it, that the notion came to comfort me of writing the Message at the top of the paper, and of committing it in the bottle to the sea. Drowning men, they say, catch at straws—and the straw of comfort I caught at was the one chance in ten thousand, that the Message might float till it was picked up, and that it might reach you. My mind might, or might not, have been failing me, by this time—but it is true, either way, that I did feel comforted when I had emptied one of the two bottles left in the medicine-chest, had put the paper inside, had tied the stopper carefully over with the oilskin, and had laid the whole by in my pocket, ready, when I felt my time coming, to drop into the sea. I was rid of the secret, I thought to myself; and, if it pleased God, I was rid of it, Alfred, to you.

The day waned; and the sun set, all cloudless and golden, in a dead calm. There was not a ripple anywhere on the long oily heaving of the sea. Before night came I strengthened myself with a better meal than usual, as to food —for where was the use of keeping meat and biscuit when I had not water enough to last along with them? When the stars came out and the moon rose, I gathered the wood together and lit the signal-fire, according to custom, on the beach outside my cavern. I had no hope from it—but the fire was company to me: the looking into it quieted my thoughts, and the crackling of it was a relief in the silence. I don't know why it was, but the breathless stillness of that night had something awful in it, and went near to frightening me.

The moon got high in the heavens, and the light of her lay all in a flood on the sand before me, on the rocks that jutted out from it, and on the calm sea beyond. I was thinking of Margaret—wondering if the moon was shining on our little bay at Steepways, and if she was looking at it too—when I saw a man's shadow steal over the white of the sand. He was lurking near me again! In a minute, he came into view. The moonshine glinted on his blue spectacles, and glimmered on his bald head. He stooped as he passed by the rocks and looked about for a loose stone: he found a large one, and came straight with it on tiptoe, up to the fire. I showed myself to him on a sudden, in the red of the flame, with the pistol in my hand. He dropped the stone, and shrank back, at the sight of it. When he was close to the sea, he stopped, and screamed out at me, "The ship's coming! The ship's coming! The ship shall never find you!" That notion of the ship, and that other notion of killing me before help came to us, seemed never to have left him. When he turned, and went back by the way he had come, he was still shouting out those same words. For a quarter of an hour or more, I heard him, till the silence swallowed

up his ravings, and led me back again to my thoughts of home.

Those thoughts kept with me, till the moon was on the wane. It was darker now, and stiller than ever. I had not fed the signal-fire for half an hour or more, and had roused myself up, at the mouth of the cavern, to do it, when I saw the dying gleams of moonshine over the sea on either side of me change colour, and turn red. Black shadows, as from low-flying clouds, swept after each other over the deepening redness. The air grew hot—a sound came nearer and nearer, from above me and behind me, like the rush of wind and the roar of water, both together, and both far off. I ran out on to the sand, and looked back. The island was on fire!

On fire at the point of it opposite to me—on fire in one great sheet of flame that stretched right across the island, and bore down on me steadily before the light westerly wind which was blowing at the time. Only one hand could have kindled that terrible flame—the hand of the lost wretch who had left me, with the mad threat on his lips and the murderous notion of burning me out of my refuge, working in his crazy brain. On his side of the island (where the fire had begun), the dry grass and scrub grew all round the little hollow in the earth which I had left to him for his place of refuge. If he had had a thousand lives to lose, he would have lost that thousand already!

Having nothing to feed on but the dry scrub, the flame swept forward with such a frightful swiftness, that I had barely time, after mastering my own scattered senses, to turn back into the cavern to get my last drink of water and my last mouthful of food, before I heard the fiery scorch crackling over the thatched-roof which my own hands had raised. I ran across the beach to the spur of rock which jutted out into the sea, and there crouched down on the farthest edge I could reach to. There was nothing for the fire to lay hold of between me and the top of the island-bank. I was far enough away to be out of the lick of the flames, and low enough down to get air under the sweep of the smoke. You may well wonder why, with death by starvation threatening me close at hand, I should have schemed and struggled as I did, to save myself from a quicker death by suffocation in the smoke. I can only answer to that, that I wonder too—but so it was.

The flames eat their way to the edge of the bank, and lapped over it as if they longed to lick me up. The heat scorched nearer than I had thought, and the smoke poured lower and thicker. I lay down sick and weak on the rock, with my face close over the calm cool water. When I ventured to lift myself up again, the top of the island was of a ruby red, the smoke rose slowly in little streams, and the air above was quivering with the heat. While I looked at it, I felt a kind of surging and singing in my head, and a deadly faintness and coldness crept all over me. I took the bottle that held the Message from my pocket, and dropped it into the sea—then crawled a little way back over the rocks, and fell forward on them before I could get as far as the sand. The last I remember was trying to say my prayers—losing the words—losing my sight—losing the sense of where I was—losing everything.

The day was breaking again, when I was roused up by feeling rough hands on me. Naked savages—some on the rocks, some in the water, some in two long canoes—were clamouring and crowding about on all sides. They bound me, and took me off at once to one of the canoes. The other kept company—and both were paddled back to that high land which I had seen in the south. Death had passed me by once more—and Captivity had come in its place.

The story of my life among the savages, having no concern with the matter now in hand, may be passed by here in few words. They had seen the fire on the island; and paddling over to reconnoitre, had found me. Not one of them had ever set eyes on a white man before. I was taken away to be shown about among them for a curiosity. When they were tired of showing me, they spared my life, finding my knowledge and general handiness as a civilised man useful to them in various ways. I lost all count of time in my captivity—and can only guess now that it lasted more than one year and less than two. I made two attempts to escape, each time in a canoe, and was balked in both. Nobody at home in England would ever, as I believe, have seen me again, if an outward-bound vessel had not touched at the little desert island for fresh water. Finding none there, she came on to the territory of the savages (which was an island too). When they took me on board, I looked little better than a savage myself, and could hardly talk my own language. By the help of the kindness shown to me, I was right again by the time we spoke the first ship homeward-bound. To that vessel I was transferred; and, in her, I worked my passage back to Falmouth.

CHAPTER V. THE RESTITUTION.

CAPTAIN JORGAN, up and out betimes, had put the whole village of Lanrean under an amicable cross-examination, and was returning to the King Arthur's Arms to breakfast, none the wiser for his trouble, when he beheld the young fisherman advancing to meet him, accompanied by a stranger. A glance at this stranger, assured the captain that he could be no other than the Seafaring Man; and the captain was about to hail him as a fellow-craftsman, when the two stood still and silent before the captain, and the captain stood still silent, and wondering before them.

"Why, what's this!" cried the captain, when at last he broke the silence. "You two are alike. You two are much alike! What's this!"

Not a word was answered on the other side, until after the seafaring brother had got hold of the captain's right hand, and the fisherman brother had got hold of the captain's left hand; and if ever the captain had had his fill of hand-shaking, from his birth to that hour, he had it

then. And presently up and spoke the two brothers, one at a time, two at a time, two dozen at a time for the bewilderment into which they plunged the captain, until he gradually had Hugh Raybrock's deliverance made clear to him, and also unravelled the fact that the person referred to in the half-obliterated paper, was Tregarthen himself.

"Formerly, dear Captain Jorgan," said Alfred, "of Lanrean, you recollect? Kitty and her father came to live at Steepways, after Hugh shipped on his last voyage."

"Ay, ay!" cried the captain, fetching a breath. "Now you have me in tow. Then your brother here, don't know his sister-in-law that is to be, so much as by name?"

"Never saw her; never heard of her!"

"Ay, ay, ay!" cried the captain. "Why, then we every one go back together—paper, writer, and all—and take Tregarthen into the secret we kept from him?"

"Surely," said Alfred, "we can't help it now. We must go through with our duty."

"Not a doubt," returned the captain. "Give me an arm apiece, and let us set this ship-shape."

So, walking up and down in the shrill wind on the wild moor, while the neglected breakfast cooled within, the captain and the brothers settled their course of action.

It was, that they should all proceed by the quickest means they could secure, to Barnstaple, and there look over the father's books and papers in the lawyer's keeping: as Hugh had proposed to himself to do, if ever he reached home. That, enlightened or unenlightened, they should then return to Steepways and go straight to Mr. Tregarthen, and tell him all they knew, and see what came of it, and act accordingly. Lastly, that when they got there, they should enter the village with all precautions against Hugh's being recognised by any chance; and that to the captain should be consigned the task of preparing his wife and mother for his restoration to this life.

"For, you see," quoth Captain Jorgan, touching the last head, "it requires caution any way; great joys being as dangerous as great griefs—if not more dangerous, as being more uncommon (and therefore less provided against) in this round world of ours. And besides, I should like to free my name with the ladies, and take you home again at your brightest and luckiest; so don't let's throw away a chance of success."

The captain was highly lauded by the brothers for his kind interest and foresight.

"And now, stop!" said the captain, coming to a stand-still, and looking from one brother to the other, with quite a new rigging of wrinkles about each eye; "you are of opinion," to the elder, "that you are ra'ather slow?"

"I assure you I am very slow," said the honest Hugh.

"Wa'al," replied the captain, "I assure you that to the best of my belief I am ra'ather smart. Now, a slow man ain't good at quick business; is he?"

That was clear to both.

"You," said the captain, turning to the younger brother, "are a little in love; ain't you?"

"Not a little, Captain Jorgan."

"Much or little, you're sort preoccupied; ain't you?"

It was impossible to be denied.

"And a sort preoccupied man, ain't good at quick business; is he?" said the captain.

Equally clear on all sides.

"Now," said the captain, "I ain't in love myself, and I've made many a smart run across the ocean, and I should like to carry on and go ahead with this affair of yours and make a run slick through it. Shall I try? Will you hand it over to me?"

They were both delighted to do so, and thanked him heartily.

"Good," said the captain, taking out his watch. "This is half-past eight A.M., Friday morning. I'll jot that down, and we'll compute how many hours we've been out, when we run into your mother's post-office. There! The entry's made, and now we go ahead."

They went ahead so well, that before the Barnstaple lawyer's office was open next morning, the captain was sitting whistling on the step of the door, waiting for the clerk to come down the street with his key and open it. But, instead of the clerk, there came the master: with whom the captain fraternised on the spot, to an extent that utterly confounded him.

As he personally knew both Hugh and Alfred, there was no difficulty in obtaining immediate access to such of the father's papers as were in his keeping. These were chiefly old letters and cash accounts: from which the captain, with a shrewdness and despatch that left the lawyer far behind, established with perfect clearness, by noon, the following particulars.

That, one Lawrence Clissold had borrowed of the deceased, at a time when he was a thriving young tradesman in the town of Barnstaple, the sum of five hundred pounds. That, he had borrowed it, on the written statement that it was to be laid out in furtherance of a speculation, which he expected would raise him to independence: he being, at the time of writing that letter, no more than a clerk in the house of Dringworth Brothers, America-square, London. That, the money was borrowed for a stipulated period; but that when the term was out, the aforesaid speculation had failed, and Clissold was without means of repayment. That, hereupon, he had written to his creditor, in no very persuasive terms, vaguely requesting further time. That, the creditor had refused this concession, declaring that he could not afford delay. That, Clissold then paid the debt, accompanying the remittance of the money, with an angry letter, describing it as having been advanced by a relative to save him from ruin. That, in acknowledging the receipt, Raybrock had cautioned Clissold to seek to borrow money of him no more, as he would never so risk money again.

Before the lawyer, the captain said never a word in reference to these discoveries. But when the papers had been put back in their box, and he and his two companions were well out of the office, his right leg suffered for it, and he said:

"So far, this run's begun with a fair wind and a prosperous—for don't you see that all this agrees with that dutiful trust in his father, maintained by the slow member of the Raybrock family?"

Whether the brothers had seen it before or no, they saw it now. Not that the captain gave them much time to contemplate the state of things at their case, for he instantly whipped them into a chaise again, and bore them off to Steepways. Although the afternoon was but just beginning to decline when they reached it, and it was broad daylight, still they had no difficulty, by dint of muffling the returned sailor up, and ascending the village rather than descending it, in reaching Tregarthen's cottage unobserved. Kitty was not visible, and they surprised Tregarthen sitting writing in the small bay-window of his little room.

"Sir," said the captain, instantly shaking hands with him, pen and all, "I'm glad to see you, sir. How do you do, sir? I told you you'd think better of me by-and-by, and I congratulate you on going to do it."

Here, the captain's eye fell on Tom Pettifer Ho, engaged in preparing some cookery at the fire.

"That crittur," said the captain, smiting his leg, "is a born steward, and never ought to have been in any other way of life. Stop where you are, Tom, and make yourself useful. Now, Tregarthen, I'm agoing to try a chair."

Accordingly, the captain drew one close to him, and went on:

"This loving member of the Raybrock family you know, sir. This slow member of the same family, you don't know, sir. Wa'al, these two are brothers—fact! Hugh's come to life again, and here he stands. Now, see here, my friend! You don't want to be told that he was cast away, but you do want to be told (for there's a purpose in it) that he was cast away with another man. That man, by name, was Lawrence Clissold."

At the mention of this name, Tregarthen started and changed colour. "What's the matter?" said the captain.

"He was a fellow-clerk of mine, thirty—five-and-thirty—years ago."

"True," said the captain, immediately catching at the clue: "Dringworth Brothers, America-square, London City."

The other started again, nodded, and said, "That was the House."

"Now," pursued the captain, "between those two men cast away, there arose a mystery concerning the round sum of five hundred pound."

Again Tregarthen started and changed colour. Again the captain said, "What's the matter?"

As Tregarthen only answered, "Please to go on," the captain recounted, very tersely and plainly, the nature of Clissold's wanderings on the barren island, as he had condensed them in his mind from the seafaring man. Tregarthen became greatly agitated during this recital, and at length exclaimed :

"Clissold was the man who ruined me! I have suspected it for many a long year, and now I know it."

"And how," said the captain, drawing his chair still closer to Tregarthen, and clapping his hand upon his shoulder, "how may you know it?"

"When we were fellow-clerks," replied Tregarthen, "in that London House, it was one of my duties to enter daily in a certain book, an account of the sums received that day by the firm, and afterwards paid into the banker's. One memorable day—a Wednesday, the black day of my life—among the sums I so entered, was one of five hundred pounds."

"I begin to make it out," said the captain. "Yes?"

"It was one of Clissold's duties to copy from this entry, a memorandum of the sums which the clerk employed to go to the banker's paid in there. It was my duty to hand the money to Clissold; it was Clissold's to hand it to the clerk, with that memorandum of his writing. On that Wednesday, I entered a sum of five hundred pounds received. I handed that sum, as I handed the other sums in the day's entry, to Clissold. I was absolutely certain of it at the time; I have been absolutely certain of it ever since. A sum of five hundred pounds was afterwards found by the House to have been that day wanting from the bag, from Clissold's memorandum, and from the entries in my book. Clissold, being questioned, stood upon his perfect clearness in the matter, and emphatically declared that he asked no better than to be tested by 'Tregarthen's book.' My book was examined, and the entry of five hundred pounds was not there."

"How not there," said the captain, "when you made it yourself?"

Tregarthen continued :-

"I was then questioned. Had I made the entry? Certainly I had. The House produced my book, and it was not there. I could not deny my book; I could not deny my writing. I knew there must be forgery by some one; but the writing was wonderfully like mine, and I could impeach no one if the House could not. I was required to pay the money back. I did so, and I left the House, almost broken-hearted, rather than remain there—even if I could have done so—with a dark shadow of suspicion always on me. I returned to my native place, Lanrean, and remained there, clerk to a mine, until I was appointed to my little post here."

"I well remember," said the captain, "that I told you that if you had had no experience of ill-judgments on deceiving appearances, you were a lucky man. You were hurt at that, and I see why. I'm sorry."

"Thus it is," said Tregarthen. "Of my own innocence, I have of course been sure; it has been at once my comfort, and my trial. Of Clissold I have always had suspicions almost amounting to certainty, but they have never

been confirmed until now. For my daughter's sake and for my own, I have carried this subject in my own heart, as the only secret of my life, and have long believed that it would die with me."

"Wa'al, my good sir," said the captain, cordially, "the present question is, and will be long, I hope, concerning living, and not dying. Now, here are our two honest friends, the loving Raybrock and the slow. Here they stand, agreed on one point, on which I'd back 'em round the world, and right across it from north to south, and then again from east to west, and through it, from your deepest Cornish mine to China. It is, that they will never use this same so-often-mentioned sum of money, and that restitution of it must be made to you. These two, the loving member and the slow, for the sake of the right and of their father's memory, will have it ready for you to-morrow. Take it, and ease their minds and mine, and end a most unfort'-nate transaction."

Tregarthen took the captain by the hand, and gave his hand to each of the young men, but positively and finally answered, No. He said, they trusted to his word, and he was glad of it, and at rest in his mind—but there was no proof, and the money must remain as it was. All were very earnest over this; and earnestness in men, when they are right and true, is so impressive, that Mr. Pettifer deserted his cookery and looked on quite moved.

"And so," said the captain, "so we come—as that lawyer-crittur over yonder where we were this morning, might—to mere proof; do we? We must have it; must we? How? From this Clissold's wanderings, and from what you say, it ain't hard to make out that there was a neat forgery of your writing committed by the too smart Rowdy that was grease and ashes when I made his acquaintance, and a substitution of a forged leaf in your book for a real and true leaf torn out. Now, was that real and true leaf then and there destroyed? No—for says he, in his drunken way, he slipped it into a crack in his own desk, because you came into the office before there was time to burn it—and could never get back to it afterwards. Wait a bit. Where is that desk now? Do you consider it likely to be in America-square, London City?"

Tregarthen shook his head.

"The House has not, for years, transacted business in that place. I have heard of it and read of it, as removed, enlarged, every way altered. Things alter so fast in these times."

"You think so," returned the captain, with compassion; "but you should come over and see me, afore you talk about that. Wa'al, now. This desk, this paper—this paper, this desk," said the captain, ruminating and walking about; and looking, in his uneasy abstraction, into Mr. Pettifer's hat on a table, among other things. "This desk, this paper—this paper, this desk," the captain continued, musing and roaming about the room, "I'd give——"

However, he gave nothing, but took up his steward's hat instead, and stood looking into it, as if he had just come into Church. After that he roamed again, and again said, "This desk, belonging to this House of Dringworth Brothers, America-square, London City——"

Mr. Pettifer, still strangely moved and now more moved than before, cut the captain off as he backed across the room, and bespake him thus:

"Captain Jorgan, I have been wishful to engage your attention, but I couldn't do it. I am unwilling to interrupt, Captain Jorgan, but I must do it. I know something about that House."

The captain stood stock-still, and looked at him—with his (Mr. Pettifer's) hat under his arm.

"You're aware," pursued his steward, "that I was once in the broking business, Captain Jorgan?"

"I was aware," said the captain, "that you had failed in that calling and in half the businesses going, Tom."

"Not quite so, Captain Jorgan; but I failed in the broking business. I was partners with my brother, sir. There was a sale of old office furniture at Dringworth Brothers when the House was moved from America-square, and me and my brother made what we call in the trade a Deal there, sir. And I'll make bold to say, sir, that the only thing I ever had from my brother, or from any relation—for my relations have mostly taken property from me, instead of giving me any—was an old desk we bought at that same sale, with a crack in it. My brother wouldn't have given me even that, when we broke partnership, if it had been worth anything."

"Where is that desk now?" said the captain.

"Well, Captain Jorgan," replied the steward, "I couldn't say for certain where it is now; but when I saw it last—which was last time we were outward-bound—it was at a very nice lady's at Wapping, along with a little chest of mine which was detained for a small matter of a bill owing."

The captain, instead of paying that rapt attention to his steward which was rendered by the other three persons present, went to Church again, in respect of the steward's hat. And a most especially agitated and memorable face the captain produced from it, after a short pause.

"Now, Tom," said the captain, "I spoke to you, when we first came here, respecting your constitutional weakness on the subject of sunstroke?"

"You did, sir."

"Will my slow friend," said the captain, "lend me his arm, or I shall sink right back'ards into this blessed steward's cookery?—Now, Tom," pursued the captain, when the required assistance was given, "on your oath as a steward, didn't you take that desk to pieces to make a better one of it, and put it together fresh—or something of the kind?"

"On my oath I did, sir," replied the steward.

"And by the blessing of Heaven, my friends, one and all," cried the captain, radiant with joy —"of the Heaven that put it into this Tom Pettifer's head to take so much care of his head against the bright sun—Lo! lined his hat with the

original leaf in Tregarthen's writing—and here it is!"

With that, the captain, to the utter destruction of Mr. Pettifer's favourite hat, produced the book-leaf, very much worn, but still legible, and gave both his legs such tremendous slaps, that they were heard far off in the bay, and never accounted for.

"A quarter-past five P.M.," said the captain, pulling out his watch, "and that's thirty-three hours and a quarter in all, and a pretty run!" .

How they were all overpowered with delight and triumph; how the money was restored, then and there to Tregarthen; how Tregarthen, then and there, gave it all to his daughter; how the captain undertook to go to Dringworth Brothers and re-establish the reputation of their forgotten old clerk; how Kitty came in, and was nearly torn to pieces, and the marriage was reappointed; needs not to be told. Nor, how she and the young fisherman went home to the post-office to prepare the way for the captain's coming, by declaring him to be the mightiest of men who had made all their fortunes—and then dutifully withdrew together, in order that he might have the domestic coast entirely to himself. How he availed himself of it, is all that remains to tell.

Deeply delighted with his trust, and putting his heart into it, he raised the latch of the post-office parlour where Mrs. Raybrock and the young widow sat, and said:

"May I come in?"

"Sure you may, Captain Jorgan!" replied the old lady. "And good reason you have to be free of the house, though you have not been too well used in it, by some who ought to have known better. I ask your pardon."

"No you don't, ma'am," said the captain, "for I won't let you. Wa'al to be sure!" By this time he had taken a chair on the hearth between them. "Never felt such an evil spirit in the whole course of my life! There! I tell you! I could a'most have cut my own connexion—Like the dealer in my country, away West, who when he had let himself be outdone in a bargain, said to himself, 'Now I tell you what! I'll never speak to you again.' And he never did, but joined a settlement of oysters, and translated the multiplication-table into their language. Which is a fact that can be proved. If you doubt it, mention it to any oyster you come across, and see if he'll have the face to contradict it."

He took the child from her mother's lap, and set it on his knee.

"Not a bit afraid of me now, you see. Knows I am fond of small people. I have a child, and she's a girl, and I sing to her sometimes."

"What do you sing?" asked Margaret.

"Not a long song, my dear.

Silas Jorgan
Played the organ.

That's about all. And sometimes I tell her stories. Stories of sailors supposed to be lost, and recovered after all hope was abandoned." Here the captain musingly went back to his song:

"Silas Jorgan
Played the organ,"

—repeating it with his eyes on the fire, as he softly danced the child on his knee. For, he felt that Margaret had stopped working.

"Yes," said the captain, still looking at the fire. "I make up stories and tell 'em to that child. Stories of shipwreck on desert islands and long delay in getting back to civilised lands. It is to stories the like of that, mostly, that

> Silas Jorgan
> Plays the organ."

There was no light in the room but the light of the fire; for, the shades of night were on the village, and the stars had begun to peep out of the sky one by one, as the houses of the village peeped out from among the foliage when the night departed. The captain felt that Margaret's eyes were upon him, and thought it discreetest to keep his own eyes on the fire.

"Yes; I make 'em up," said the captain. "I make up stories of brothers brought together by the good providence of GOD. Of sons brought back to mothers—husbands brought back to wives—fathers raised from the deep, for little children like herself."

Margaret's touch was on his arm, and he could not choose but look round now. Next moment her hand moved imploringly to his breast, and she was on her knees before him: supporting the mother, who was also kneeling.

"What's the matter?" said the captain. "What's the matter?

> Silas Jorgan
> Played the——"

Their looks and tears were too much for him, and he could not finish the song, short as it was.

"Mistress Margaret, you have borne ill fortune well. Could you bear good fortune equally well, if it was to come?"

"I hope so. I thankfully and humbly and earnestly hope so!"

"Wa'al, my dear," said the captain, "p'raps it has come. He's—don't be frightened—shall I say the word?"

"Alive?"

"Yes!"

The thanks they fervently addressed to Heaven were again too much for the captain, who openly took out his handkerchief and dried his eyes.

"He's no further off," resumed the captain, "than my country. Indeed, he's no further off than his own native country. To tell you the truth, he's no further off than Falmouth. Indeed, I doubt if he's quite so far. Indeed, if you was sure you could bear it nicely, and I was to do no more than whistle for him——"

The captain's trust was discharged. A rush came, and they were all together again.

This was a fine opportunity for Tom Pettifer to appear with a tumbler of cold water, and he presently appeared with it, and administered it to the ladies: at the same time soothing them, and composing their dresses, exactly as if they had been passengers crossing the Channel. The extent to which the captain slapped his legs, when Mr. Pettifer acquitted himself of this act of stewardship, could have been thoroughly appreciated by no one but himself: inasmuch as he must have slapped them black and blue, and they must have smarted tremendously.

He couldn't stay for the wedding; having a few appointments to keep, at the irreconcilable distance of about four thousand miles. So, next morning, all the village cheered him up to the level ground above, and there he shook hands with a complete Census of its population, and invited the whole, without exception, to come and stay several months with him at Salem, Mass., U.S. And there, as he stood on the spot where he had seen that little golden picture of love and parting, and from which he could that morning contemplate another golden picture with a vista of golden years in it, little Kitty put her arms around his neck, and kissed him on both his bronzed cheeks, and laid her pretty face upon his storm-beaten breast, in sight of all: ashamed to have called such a noble captain names. And there, the captain waved his hat over his head three final times; and there, he was last seen, going away accompanied by Tom Pettifer Ho, and carrying his hands in his pockets. And there, before that ground was softened with the fallen leaves of three more summers, a rosy little boy took his first unsteady run to a fair young mother's breast, and the name of that infant fisherman was Jorgan Raybrock.

THE END.

Published at the Office, No. 26, Wellington Street, Strand. Printed by C. WHITING, Beaufort House, Strand.